*Piper Pu*

# The Waiting Room

Piper Punches

Terri,
Thank you for ~~Read~~ reading
the Waiting Room. This is my
book baby! ♡

*Piper R*

## DEDICATED TO MY FAMILY

Those wonderful people in my life that never gave up on me; sticking with me no matter what to help me reach my goals.

# Part One

*Waiting rooms tell stories. They are a medical purgatory. Some sit in the waiting room for hours to be shown the light, graced with blessings like a new baby. For others, this is the final holding room before they are delivered into hell, facing uncertainty, despair, sadness, even death.*

*-Sylvie Day*

## Chapter 1 – Charlotte
*Present Day*

I had never felt so many emotions in one day. Never had I found myself sobbing guttural, disgusting sobs one minute, and feeling completely elated and awestruck the next. All day long I received strangers, childhood friends, even a random news crew at my mother's home; all of them offering condolences, adding their memories to the collection of things I didn't know about my mom, and telling me what a wonderful woman Dr. Sylvie Day had been. I listened politely and nodded accordingly, feeling at ease, yet utterly bewildered that my mother had touched the lives of hundreds of people in this small town, not to mention scores of others who mailed cards or posted social media condolences.

Each person that stepped over the threshold of my mother's two-bedroom farmhouse brought with them a symbol of their generation. The oldest of my mother's patients brought baked goods. Middle-aged women and men brought flowers or plants. The youngest visitors were teenagers, with empty hands and sullen faces, being dragged to the visitation as evidence of all the good my mother had done in this small town. After all, she had birthed at least three-fourths of them.

Of course I realized my mother was special. What child doesn't? But I didn't realize the impact that one woman could have on an entire community. When I met with Gary Reinhold of

Reinhold and Sons Funeral Home to plan the services, he alluded to her impact. He sat behind a massive pine desk that flagrantly overpowered his tiny five foot six frame – a wisp of a man that had helped countless generations lay to rest their loved ones. I wondered if he ever contemplated his own demise when he was surrounded by death all the time.

"Charlotte, I am not sure we can handle the amount of visitors who will want to pay respect to your mother. God rest her soul." The funeral home was non-denominational, but Gary crossed himself, and then wiped a tear from his eye.

"Surely you have had large services before. I don't know where else to go."

Gary nodded. "Yes, yes. Well, we will certainly take very good care of Sylvie and her interment, but might I make a suggestion?"

The suggestion had been to rent a massive tent, one of those used for joyous outdoor gatherings like weddings and graduations. It would be placed on my mother's property; 250 acres of farmland smack in the middle of rural Missouri – an area spacious enough to receive, welcome, and provide parking for the multitude of guests that Gary was sure would be arriving to pay their final respects.

It felt strange that a town with a population large enough to support a Home Depot, a Walmart, and a proposed 70 million dollar outlet mall on recently sold farmland could not support more than one funeral home. I told Gary this and he shrugged sadly. "Marion is a transitory town now. People, they come and they go, staying for a short time until better things pull them away. You understand the pull. How long have you been away?" I nodded because I couldn't argue with the truth. "Your mom is an icon in this town. People are going to show up for her funeral. They'll come from all over. Just you wait and see."

I was hesitant about the unconventional funeral arrangements, but Nick seemed to think it made perfect sense. Taking my hand as we left the funeral home to go back to mom's farmhouse to prepare, he said, "Charlie, it makes perfect sense. Your mom wouldn't want to be laid out in a cheaply decorated funeral home. She'd want to be in a place that meant something to her. It is a perfect solution; better than St. Roberts, even."

I felt a giggle tickle my throat and I smiled. Gary had mentioned St. Roberts Cathedral as another option for the service. It had undergone a massive renovation a decade or so ago and was a modern, Roman Catholic Church that could possibly rival the size of the Sistine Chapel. My self-proclaimed, agnostic mother would never have stepped foot inside. "If I choose St. Roberts my mother would haunt me for the rest of my days."

When I was little, my mom's beliefs were a blessing because it meant I didn't have to get up early for church on Sunday mornings and listen to an old and tired priest lecture about hell and damnation. Of course, I didn't know first-hand this was what happened at church. It was second-hand knowledge passed along to me by Jia Lin, my best friend, who tended to overdramatize most events

"You're so lucky," Jia would gush when she came to my house on Sunday afternoons to play with dolls or listen to Top 40 radio. "I wish my mom worked all the time so we could skip church. Boring," she said as she melodramatically rolled her eyes.

In a town as small as Marion there weren't too many people that didn't take a pause on Sunday morning to attend services. Most of Marion believed that Mom didn't attend services because she was too busy delivering God's little miracles into the world. Not because she wasn't sure God existed. My mom, a woman who never held back her opinions, was perfectly content to let people believe what they wanted. This puzzled me. Why would she lie?

"Oh, Charlotte, I have my reasons for not being sure about God. If I let other people know I felt that way, they would just try to convince me otherwise. I don't need to be convinced, guided, or shown the light. Let people think what they want and all will be fine with the world."

"Don't you think the babies you help deliver are miracles from a greater power?" I asked.

Mom smiled up at me. By then I was thirteen and at least three inches taller than her). "I certainly think you're a miracle."

I smiled at that memory as Nick opened the car door for me.

\*\*\*

Gary was right. People began showing up first thing at nine the next morning. I had just finished washing out my coffee cup at the kitchen sink when I looked up and saw the line of cars beginning to snake along the property. The farmhouse sat right in the middle of the property, which meant you had to drive along a dirt road for several minutes before you made it to the house. It seemed so remote for 21$^{st}$ century living, but Mom loved it.

"Privacy," she always said. "These days no one takes privacy seriously, but I do. This is my retreat. I don't want to make it easy for people to intrude on us."

The trail of cars was impressive. It reminded me of the scene in Field of Dreams when visitors are being drawn to the ball field that Kevin Costner's character built. *If you build it they will come.* Gary had been right; there is no way that his funeral home could have handled this crowd.

Nick came up behind me, putting his strong hands on my shoulders. In that moment, I loved him more than ever. Just his presence was enough to calm me. He whistled slowly. "Wow. I hope we have enough food." We both turned to look at the measly cheese and meat spread that sat on the island waiting to be taken outside.

It turned out that it didn't matter. Everyone who embarked upon the farmhouse and gathered outside under the tent brought food – tons of food. So much food that the deep freeze Mom had in the basement couldn't accommodate it all. As I packed away the last casserole that would fit, I wondered if we'd be able to find a shelter to take the excess without offending anyone.

The stream of visitors persisted all day, the line of traffic never ceasing. There was never a lull. Never a chance to stop, catch a breath, and regroup. Receiving hundreds of guests was exhausting. There wasn't even time to retreat to the bathroom to search for Tylenol or something else to dull the headache that had begun to keep a steady beat near my right temple. I couldn't imagine what it would have been like if the visitation had been at the funeral home; standing in one place, the line never ending. At least doing it this way (because it had to be done, there was no one else that this sad, sullen task could fall to) Nick and I were able to mingle, move, and occasionally sit.

At one point early in day I caught sight of mom's casket resting underneath the gargantuan tent adjacent to the farmhouse, surrounded by a mob of people. Yet the scene was terribly lonely. I knew she was there, but she really wasn't. Tears assembled behind my eyes as I remembered the only time that my mom had wanted to host a party on this land. This was her sanctuary. She rarely even entertained close friends at the house. The only time she had offered up her privacy was when Nick and I had announced our engagement.

"Why not have your wedding here?" she had asked.

"Here?" I responded, incredulously. We had been sitting on the front porch, sipping tea out of tea cups that were someday meant to be handed down to me – china with a pink and white rosette print that was way too dainty for my urbanized tastes. It was a rare autumn day when the temperatures soared into the upper 80s. I laughed. "Why here? Do you know how many people would be trampling through the yard, mistreating your rose bushes?"

"It's a big space. You could have the wedding of your dreams," she debated. "I mean look, Charlotte. Look how much land to host a grand party for all of your friends and Nick's friends, his family." My mother gestured to the rolling fields of green that had begun to turn brown as the season progressed without a drop of rain. I couldn't bring myself to tell her that I had always been aware of how incredibly large the property was. I couldn't find a non-hurtful way of saying that I had felt trapped by its vastness for so many years, sitting in the two bedroom farmhouse unable to escape; it was an island that was surrounded by green fields of soy beans, corn, and redundancy.

"You would save so much money. To rent a space this big in Chicago would cost a fortune and you wouldn't have the scenery," she continued.

I shook my head. "Nick and I don't need a big space. He has a small family, too. Besides we weren't considering a wedding in the city anyway. We are thinking a sunset wedding in Aruba on the beach."

Mom sighed and nodded. One of her greatest qualities was not enforcing her will, although I must admit there were times when one could mistake this for not caring enough. "Yes, yes; you and your beach. You have always been drawn to the water. I understand. I just thought that by getting married here your father would, in a way, be there too."

I remembered taking mom's hands; they had begun to feel old; ropey and veiny. "He is, Mom. Right here." I brought her hands to my heart and we shared a smile.

***

"Oh, and your momma and I laughed so hard we damned near peed our knickers." Mabel Schulte cackled and squeezed my leg as she reminisced about the time that she and my mom had discovered Mabel's brother, Harold, sitting ten feet below the ground in slush and human waste. "We done told Mr. Smarty Pants that the outhouse was in bad shape, but he wouldn't listen to nothin' your Momma and I told him. Born two minutes ahead of me and he thought he always knew better. I tell you. Sylvie swore that from that day he was transformed. The waste acted like a potion that turned him into the sour nutter that he is today."

Mabel looked across the way, squinting in the sunlight. I followed her gaze and saw Harold standing alone by the growing assortment of food under a second tent that had just been brought in to shield the mounting number of mourners from the midday sun. "I take it your brother isn't the friendly type, huh?"

Mabel shrugged. After 78 years there isn't much you can say to defend someone who had continued to disappoint and alienate people, even if that person is your own flesh and blood. "My brother didn't need to fall in a vat of shit to repel people. He seemed to have an aura of stink around him from the time he was a boy. But, aside from his Isabel, I reckon he always held a soft spot for your Momma."

I raised my eyebrows at this statement. "That's a curious thought. The only memory I have of my mom interacting with him is when she stood on that front porch with my Granddad's rifle, telling him to get off her land."

Mabel giggled and placed her hand atop my own, patting lightly; the liver spots sprinkled across the tops like confetti. "Life is complicated, you know. I suppose death brings the peace. I sure did love your momma so, even as we drifted apart over the years."

We sat there like that for some time; me contemplating whether or not death was peaceful even during times when it occurred so violently. What was Mabel thinking? I couldn't know. I could only guess that she may have been contemplating her own rapidly approaching mortality.

\*\*\*

It's hard for me to imagine having any other mother than my mom. From the time I was little I knew she was special. It wasn't the way that she sang her own rendition of classic lullabies to lull me back to sleep after a fierce Midwest thunderstorm. It wasn't the way that she comforted me when Bobby Cullins called me "the turd-faced daughter of a Negro lover" when mom came to the aid of a young African-American woman who had been left to fend for herself, alone and pregnant. It wasn't the way that mom looked after me that made me realize the depth of her worth not only as a mother, but a human being. No, it was the way that she looked after the women that lived, breathed, and sometimes died in Marion.

Mom was a pioneer in this small town. When she returned to Marion after earning her medical degree in St. Louis, the population was only about 400 people. Some people may have believed she was nothing more than a glorified midwife, but those few, far, and in between criticisms didn't deter her from doing what she was trained to do; take care of women, their bodies, and their babies.

Back in those days, the late 1960s, the rest of the country might have been all about peace, love, and equality, but in Marion people's ways were hard to change. It took a while for Mom to be looked upon as the healer that she was. Her first waiting room was the front parlor of our farmhouse, long before I was born.

"What's voodoo?" I asked her one day when I was about five. It had been a rare Sunday when it was just her and I. Nobody was requesting her appearance to bring a new life into the world. Usually, I spent Sundays with Granny and Granddad at their house, which was technically on our farm but a couple of acres enough away that we didn't see them every day.

We were working in the garden, getting it ready to plant the first crops of the spring. By that time the farm was no longer a working farm, just miles and miles of land to be admired for its purity. The only farming we did was in a 12 foot by 12 foot plot in our backyard.

"Voodoo? Where did you hear that word?" Mom smiled as she dropped a pea seed into the tiny hole she had poked into the soft earth.

"Bobby Cullins," I replied. Bobby Cullins would be the bane of my existence for years. I just didn't know it yet. I heard Mom sigh, but she didn't respond. "So," I prodded. "What is it?"

"It's a type of spiritual magic that people from other cultures embrace as a way to another spiritual pathway." Mom had a way of speaking to me like I was her equal, even when I was too young to really understand what she was saying.

"Bobby says people use voodoo to hurt people."

"I guess people can use their thoughts or their religion to hurt people, but not in magical ways."

"Bobby says that his daddy says that you do voodoo when you help people."

Mom sighed again. Years later she would tell me that Bobby Cullins' dad had been a dim-witted asshole who believed women were merely meant to cower to a man's will. But that day she simply asked, "What do you think?"

I stopped my planting and looked up at Mom, her face a shadow as the sun shone behind her, illuminating her already fiery red hair, the same red hair that I had. I remember feeling the love spread through my body. I climbed into her lap, dirty and smelling like damp earth. "I love you, Mommy."

She held me tight and rocked me back in forth as we sat in the garden. "I love you, too."

** *

"Charlotte?" the voice crept up behind me. By instinct I touched the back of my neck, running my fingers along the ridge of a scar that still tingled when I heard that voice, while my other hand touched my stomach. I turned slowly, willing myself to stand steady. I searched the crowd for Nick, but couldn't find him among the masses.

"Bobby." Unlike the majority of people in Marion, he hadn't aged much since the last time I saw him, a few months after high school graduation. The true townies, those who lived and died in Marion, tended to grow wider as the years passed. Their hair seemed to fade and they wore the hardships that farming can do to a soul on their faces. Not Bobby. He still looked the same nearly 20 years later. He must have gotten away from this town, too.

He tucked his hands into his pants pockets and regarded me with uncertainty. "Sorry to hear about your mom."

"Hmmm," that was all I had managed to say. I had better manners, but I couldn't conjure them at that moment.

"Thank you," Nick said for me. I closed my eyes and thanked

Mom. She must have seen Bobby coming and sent Nick to rescue me because she couldn't. Nick took his place beside me and stared uncompromising at Bobby Cullins. For a moment I entertained a random thought. *I wonder if he goes by Robert now.*

I started to excuse myself when a tow-headed child of no older than three came running past me, nearly knocking me to the ground. The little girl grabbed onto Bobby's legs and began tugging on his tailored pants. "This here is Annabelle," Bobby said, picking her up.

I tightened my grip on Nick's hand. He answered for me, us. "A beautiful little girl you have there."

Bobby nodded in agreement. The air was thick, chock-full of history and boiling with tension. I hadn't given much thought to him showing up here. It wasn't a secret that he wasn't my mom's favorite person (or mine) and he had rarely shown her much respect all those years ago. I suppose that people could change as the years wore on, growing into compassionate and decent human beings. But that scar still tingled, telling me to let Bobby and the past go. He had paid his respects and now it was time to leave.

"So, Charlotte," he started. "I was wondering if we could talk. I need to," he looked at Nick with uncertainty. "I wanted to apologize."

I found my voice. It came out gravely as if I hadn't muttered a word in all of my 36 years. "I think some things are best left alone."

"Maybe, but this matters too much. The way I treated you was wrong."

"I appreciate the sentiment, Bobby, but this isn't the place and I think it will do everyone well to leave the past where it belongs." I stared at that little girl whose almond-shaped brown eyes were staring at me too intently. "You do have a beautiful daughter."

*** 

The day had stretched itself out as long as it could. It seemed that the sun was unwilling to let Mom go, too. The visitors stayed until the sun bobbled just over the horizon; the last one to leave was Harold Klein. He hobbled over to me, leaning on his hand-carved cane with his hat in his hand. He seemed weak, defeated, and not like the man I remembered from all of those years past when he had stood on our front porch with the barrel of a gun lodged underneath his chin.

"Charlotte, I would ask how the day does you, but I suppose circumstances can speak for themselves." He didn't say the words unkindly. In fact, his voice seemed to catch as if he were holding back some complicated emotions I didn't really understand.

We stood next to the casket. I ran my hand over the polished wood wondering where my mother was. Not being a faithful person myself, I felt empty and unsure. Maybe if I had gone to church with Jia a few times I would have felt fulfilled and at peace knowing my mom was dancing in fields of gold, my father welcoming her with open arms. Then again maybe I wouldn't. "It's been a long day."

Harold nodded. "Yes. Yes, it has."

"You've been here for a long time, Mr. Klein. You must be tired."

"Live this long, dear, and everything will make you tired." He reached into his suit and pulled out an envelope. "I wanted to wait until everyone had left. You know how these places are. Towns like this. People like to talk."

I reached out to take the envelope, but he didn't let go right away. "You've turned out all right, I suppose – a spitting image of Sylvie. I'm sure you made her proud."

A smile tugged at the corners of my mouth even though his compliment was awkward. I hoped this was true. Mom and I were so different and some of the choices I had made haunted me. I wanted to believe that I hadn't failed her. Harold released his hold on the envelope and placed his hat on his head.

"Well, goodnight Charlotte. Read that over tonight. It's important. I will see you soon."

I watched him hobble off as Nick came up beside me. "What was that all about?"

I took a closer look at the letter and saw my mom's handwriting. The letter was addressed to me. We went inside the farmhouse and sat down in the living room in front of the fireplace. I wished it was colder. It was too hot to consider a fire, but I had always felt comforted by the crackling embers when we would fire up the fireplace during the winter months. Nick sat behind me on the tattered red couch and rubbed my shoulders. That couch was one of the few purchases my mom had made that wasn't a hand-me down. She never believed in buying something when you could reuse something else. She had been eco-friendly long before it was trendy.

As I opened the letter, I saw my mom's badly slanted writing. A leftie, her words always pulled to the left.

> *Dearest Charlotte,*
>
> *In death life is revealed. Those left behind continue to tell the story. Memories and truths spill unrestrained. Death brings peace, but sometimes chaos. Never underestimate the power of truth over those who are living.*
>
> *Waiting rooms tell stories. They are a medical purgatory. Some sit in the waiting room for hours to be shown the light, graced with blessings like a new baby. For others this is the final holding room before they are delivered into hell, facing uncertainty, despair, sadness, even death. I spent my life opening the door to the waiting room; delivering a person's fate, dressed in a white coat, burdened by their pain, elated by their joy. I hid in that waiting room, too. I let the waiting room consume me and my failures.*
>
> *There are still some stories left to tell. Unfortunately, if you are receiving this letter it is because I haven't been able to tell them to you. You need to know these stories because they are part of your life. Know that I love you more than my life. I am happy and at peace.*

*Always in Your Heart,*
*Mom*


At the bottom of the letter was a post-it note with instructions:

*Meet me in the waiting room tomorrow. 9 am. Regards – Harold Klein*

My hand trembled slightly as I handed the letter to Nick. "What do you think this means?" he asked.

I had an uneasy feeling. "I don't know," I whispered.

Nick slid down to sit next to me, encircling me in his arms. He rested his chin on my head and I closed my eyes. I loved moments like this when I felt protected. Too many times in my life I had felt vulnerable. "So, what do we do?"

"I guess we put this day to rest and then face tomorrow."

## Chapter 2 – Harold
### *1945*

She sat on the side of his front porch kicking her feet back and forth against the lattice that covered the crawl space. Clack. Clack. Clack. She kept staring at him, squinting into the sun and wrinkling her nose.

"You sure are one foul smelling creature." She laughed at her stupid joke.

He didn't say anything. Instead he plunged his hand into the bucket of well water to wet the bar of lye soap he was using to scrub the filth off his body. God blessed outhouse had decided to devour him when he was using it as a hideout. He should have known better than to play hide and seek with a bunch of sissy girls. That was just asking for trouble.

"I don't think it's working." Sylvie spoke in a singsong way as her feet continued to clack, clack, clack.

"Why don't you just go home?"

Sylvie shrugged. He looked up in the back window and saw Mabel sticking her tongue out at him, making crazy eyes. *Great*, he thought, *they trapped me inside and out*. Sylvie stopped mocking him for a while, but she didn't stop watching him. Nope. She sat there staring at him and fiddling with that nasty rag doll that she dragged with her everywhere.

It wasn't even a proper rag doll. It was more of a shit brown glob. Of course, Harold only knew what a proper rag doll looked like because Mabel had a whole bureau filled with them. That nasty thing didn't resemble anything close to Mabel's exquisitely designed dolls. But it wasn't like Sylvie could afford a proper doll. With her pops unable to secure steady work and with little skill to promote, it didn't look like she would ever be able to carry anything other than a shit brown glob. As he considered this he almost felt sorry for her. Then she opened her big mouth.

"Hear you been skinning cats."

"So?" He quickly stole a glance at the lattice, remembering that a couple of his trophies were rotting under there.

"You aren't worried about getting caught?"

He scrubbed at his skin harder. It didn't seem to make a difference. If anything it rubbed the filth into his skin even deeper, creating a deeper stink. "By who? You?"

"Anyone. Jimmy Barnes' cat went missing two nights ago. Saw him putting up flyers after he attended services this morning. He was nearly crying every time he asked if anyone had seen his precious Muttons."

"What kind of name is that for a cat?"

"A proper name."

He shrugged. "Mind your business, Sylvie."

"It's just wrong, Harold. Don't it make you sad to take a life? Take something that don't belong to you?"

Why didn't she just shut up? "Ain't my concern. Just a dumb animal. What you eat on your plate every night? You don't think that's the same?"

"It ain't the same, Harold. You better change your ways or you always gonna stink like shit."

With that she catapulted off the porch, letting that poor excuse of a rag doll bounce against her legs as she walked away. Sylvie Gold was nothing but a sour apple. She always looked at him with disdain like he wasn't any better than the dirt on her shoe, when she was the one who came from squalor and bad pedigree. Still he knew she had a point and it bugged him. Skinning cats was wrong. He knew he was breaking the commandments, but what else did a ten-year-old boy have to do?

Something else bothered him lately about the way Sylvie looked at him. Usually her meanie stares and uppity attitude didn't bother him, but something was changing. He found that it aggravated him that he cared what she thought. He even found himself experiencing the sensation that a million butterflies were fluttering around inside his stomach. He had considered confiding in Mabel about these weird sensations, but at the last second decided against it. Even then he knew it was better to suppress any feelings he had about Sylvie Gold.

In the summer of 1945 Harold Klein wanted nothing more than to play baseball. His dad bought him a signed Lou Gehrig ball at an auction on one of his business trips and he spent hours tossing it up in the air as high as he could and then running as fast as he could to catch it. He had no doubt that he would make the greatest outfielder the game had ever seen. Even though he knew girls didn't play baseball (although he suspected Sylvie might) he had even entertained the thought of asking Mabel to play catch with him, but that would be nothing but a waste of time. It was times like this when he wished he had been born the twin of a brother, not a stupid girl like Mabel because if the truth were to be told, Harold had a hard time making friends. He didn't have enough friends to make up a team much less to play catch with.

"Where are all your friends, son?" his father had asked one day when they headed down to Main Street after church.

Harold shrugged and drank his soda pop at the bar while his dad mingled with the businessmen and townsfolk of Marion. Harold hated Sundays. These were the days he was forced to face people. It wasn't that he didn't like people; they just didn't seem to care for him. He was awkward and shy. Not anywhere near as outgoing and personable as Harold Klein Sr., attorney at law. It wasn't that he didn't try to make friends; he just could never stomach enough interest in the same things as the boys his age. In a small town like Marion if you didn't care about county fairs, the price of corn, and whether or not it was a good growing season then you were considered an outcast.

Harold did have one person he could consider a friend of sorts. Bart Cullins. Bart Cullins was not the kind of friend that good, God fearing boys hung out with, though. Bart Cullins was what most people would consider white trash. Then again many people considered Sylvie's pop white trash and Mabel still hung out around her. Harold figured things were different for girls.

"That Bart Cullins is not someone you should be hanging around with," Harold Sr. had mentioned the day Bart showed up at the house nosing around like he was looking for unsecured points of entry for future reference. The Cullins had a mean streak; perhaps some genetic default. There weren't too many people willing to get tangled up with that clan. *Maybe that is why I chose Bart to be my friend*, Harold reasoned. *We are both outcasts in a community that breeds intolerance.*

"He's my friend," Harold protested. The senior Harold didn't seem to have the heart to protest. Knowing that his son struggled to make friends, who was he to deny him this friendship? Of course, there was a perfectly good reason; especially if he knew that Bart was introducing his son to sadistic activities – like skinning cats.

The first time it disgusted Harold. As Bart began skinning it alive, the cat started to howl and whither under the blade. Harold couldn't bear it and he threw up all over his shoes. Bart merely laughed, shaking his head.

Harold had wiped the vomit dribble off his lips with the back of his hand, taking deep breaths. He looked around, suddenly very much aware that while they were behind Bart's house, they were still out in the open, clearly visible to anyone passing by. Bart lived in a two-bedroom shack adjacent to the hustle and bustle of Main Street. His home was observable by anyone interested in casting a scornful glance at the residence – as they often did. "Someone's gonna see,"

Harold whispered, trying not to lose what was left of his stomach contents.

Bart laughed. It was a bottomless laugh that sounded like it belonged to a criminally insane man – not a 10 year old boy. "Who cares? Besides, most people stay away from here. They know what's good for them." He waved the knife and laughed again.

"Your turn." He handed Harold the knife and gestured to the cat that lay withering at his feet.

"I don't want to," Harold asserted.

"Come on. It's just a cat."

Peer pressure was a social disease, even in 1945. What choice did Harold have? It was either submit to this cruel act or risk being ridiculed, denounced, and possibly skinned alive himself. No, there really was no choice. He had to do it.

Why Harold had *continued* to do it he couldn't say. It had been four months since he crossed that line with Bart for the first time. But he took no pleasure in skinning those cats. In fact, he cried each and every time he did it. Sylvie was right. What he did was much different than what the butchers did when the cattlemen bought their meat in to be processed. He was killing. They were surviving.

Harold believed in a way he was surviving, too, although *what* he was surviving, he wasn't quite sure. It wasn't as if his life was all that difficult. He lived comfortably with his father, mother, and Mabel. They always had food on the table. His parents weren't angry or hostile to each other or to their children. Their house wasn't like other houses where poverty and hostility went hand in hand. No, Harold didn't have much to feel sorry about. Yet he felt like each day was a struggle – a struggle to find his place in a community where he didn't feel at home.

*** 

The summer of 1945 seemed to last forever. The days were endless. The heat unrelenting. Everyone seemed to be having a hard time. Crops were suffering without the rain. Tempers were rising as quickly as the mercury in the thermometer. Women began to spend entire days doing nothing but sipping lemonade under the shade trees. Men forgot about the crops and spent too much time at home bothering their women. What this meant was come the New Year there were plenty of women walking around town with wide, swollen bellies.

Thankfully, Harold's mother had been spared. The heat hadn't touched their family in that way, but Sylvie's house was a different story. One day just before Thanksgiving, when Sylvie escaped from under her mother's watchful eye, Harold intentionally eavesdropped on a conversation between his sister and Sylvie.

"I think it's wonderful," Mabel had cooed.

"I guess." Sylvie responded.

"Why do you guess? Babies are so cute, cuddly, and they always smell delicious."

"Well, you don't eat babies. But, they sure need to eat."

"Oh."

Everything got quiet for a while. Then Mabel spoke again. "If you and your family need some food I am sure mother won't mind helping you out. We always have an extra loaf of bread and her jam is delicious. I'm sure mother would even let you put some food on her account at Mulligan's."

"I don't think Daddy would like that. He's proud."

"Yeah," Mabel agreed.

Harold had leaned against the wall, breathing slowly so he wouldn't be heard. Mabel had gotten use to his spying. He had to be pretty clever to elude her, but he didn't want to risk it. As Sylvie and Mabel started talking about some girl at school, Harold snuck away, but didn't stop thinking about what he'd overheard. An idea had begun to form. Maybe he could redeem himself for that cat business (which he had stopped shortly after Sylvie's intervention shamed him into doing the right thing). Perhaps he could be the person he knew he should be.

The trick was not to get caught. If Harold knew one thing it was that Gavin Gold was a proud man, just like Sylvie had said. He wouldn't take too kindly to handouts. He had survived the

Depression (barely). He would insist he could survive this.

The problem with Sylvie's pops, Harold reckoned, wasn't his lack of aptitude but mainly his inability to stop hitting the moonshine. This had cost him too many jobs, including a job working at the meat processing plant in town. Harold understood why they had to let him go. Meat grinding and intermittent soberness didn't make for a safe working environment. But being jobless and a drunk didn't put food on the table either and Sylvie's pop was a temperamental man. Not unreasonable, just a little unstable. You had to make sure you were on the right side of his mood.

That evening just before dinner, Harold snuck into the kitchen while his mother tended to one of Mabel's tantrum. Apparently, she been absently wandering about the yard and gotten one of her nice dresses caught on a splinter of wood that was sticking out of the entrance fence to their property. Now she was sniveling and carrying on. Usually, Harold would have been aggravated by this, but this time he took advantage of it.

He created a hammock with his front shirt tails and placed the bread for the evening meal into his pouch. He snatched a jar of jam from the canning pantry and, at the last second, grabbed a tea towel from the counter to wrap the contraband in when he delivered it. Next, he snuck around the side of the house to the chicken coop out back. His parents were far from the farming type, but they did keep a few chickens around for fresh eggs. Usually, there weren't eggs available this late in the day, but his mother must not have had time to collect them that morning. Two round eggs were waiting for Harold to pilfer. He wrapped everything in the tea towel and hid it underneath the crawl space. He'd take it to their house tonight when everyone was asleep.

Dinner was perplexing for Harold's mother. She stood over the stove, scratching and shaking her head. "That bread was sitting right here. I don't understand," she had said for the fifteenth time.

Harold Sr. laughed and reached across the table for a heap of mashed potatoes. "It's perfectly okay, Ellie. We all lose our mind eventually."

Harold's mother gave him a mischievous smile and waggled her finger at her husband. "I am not losing my mind. I baked two loaves of bread today. I can't imagine where the one for dinner went." This is when Mabel kicked Harold hard under the table, narrowing her eyes at him. He resisted the urge to make a face. The less attention drawn to him the better.

The Klein's house was two streets parallel to Main Street in town, which made it not quite a country house. But it backed up to a wide expanse of forest that separated the "townies" from the "countries." This is how most Marion residents referred to themselves, although visitors from larger cities like St. Louis would have found that description something to chuckle at because to these sorts of visitors the entire town was country.

Harold had begged off early after dinner complaining of a stomachache. "Hmph," Mabel had mumbled, but she left him alone. Now that it was dark the woods that separated his home from Sylvie's seemed menacing and foreboding. More than once he almost turned around and ran home, but he was determined to be the hero.

The thick blanket of forest was about two miles deep. On the other side of the towering oaks and massive maples were open fields as far as the eye could see. Sylvie's cabin sat right on the edge of the woods, where the fields and the trees met. Finally, after what must have been close to an hour of walking through the dark night he came within sight of the cabin. It was no wonder that Sylvie preferred to spend her days at his house playing with his insufferable sister. The cabin was falling apart at the seams. Although night had already fallen, it didn't prevent him from noticing the deteriorating conditions of the structure. The cabin was a poor excuse for a house. The metal roof was rusting in most places. Paint was peeling off the wood siding and there were several holes in the siding where mice and birds had begun to nest. The porch floorboards were riddled with holes too and the shutters hung crookedly off the hinges. Trash littered the yard and weeds grew up between old tires and other debris. He wondered if it even had electricity or modern conveniences like a stove or even an icebox. He marveled at how people could live without these contemporary necessities.

But a flame flickered in the window, casting a warm glow. He didn't want to get caught, so he stayed in the woods circling around the house until he found himself near the back door. He was pretty sure this was the door that led to the kitchen. If he sat the food on the single wooden step, it should be seen first thing in the morning. But then he realized a wild animal could come when he left and steal the whole lot. So he made a brave decision. He walked quietly to the back door, laid the bundle of food on the step, and knocked, hard and loud. Then he ran as fast as his feet would take him.

The next morning Harold was out in the backyard tossing a brand new ball his dad had given him. The air was unusually warm for November. He had on his heavy coat, but he was already starting to break a sweat. That's when he saw Sylvie emerge from the trees. In her hand was the bundle. Harold started to smile, proud to be recognized for his good deed, but stopped when he saw her nostrils flaring.

"Where's your sister?"

"I dunno. Why?"

"I told her not to do this." She looked down at the bundle in her hand.

"Mabel didn't do that."

"Then who? She's the only one who –" Sylvie stopped short. She glared at me. Her nostrils flared even wider. "You were eavesdropping."

"It's my house, too."

"That was a private conversation."

"What's the big deal? You needed food. I got you food. Why can't you be a normal person and just say thank you?"

"It is a big deal, Harold. This – " she held out her hands with the food bundle. "This could get us in serious trouble. My daddy ain't like yours. He's proud and angry."

"Well, I'm sorry. But I heard your momma was having that baby and you guys didn't have food. What did you expect us to do?"

"Nothing. Absolutely nothing." She shoved the bundle into his stomach. Harold refused to take it and it dropped at their feet.

"You're being downright ungrateful. If this food will help, just take it. How's your pops gonna know?"

Sylvie was silent. She bit her bottom lip and plopped down on the ground. Her pants were worn and didn't look one bit warm. She pulled her knees in to her chest, resting her chin on top of them. Harold gathered up the bundle of food. One of the eggs had cracked, its gooeyness oozing onto the ground.

"Will your pops hurt you?" Harold asked.

Sylvie shook her head. "Not on purpose. He's angry, but not really mean. I think he's angry at himself because he sucks on that stupid drink all day long. He wants to take care of us and when he can't, it makes him sad. So he drinks to not feel sad but then he feels angry. It's confusing."

Harold didn't know what to say. He didn't have experience with this type of family dynamic.

"If Daddy knows that someone took care of us and he couldn't, he'll just keep drinking."

"But you can't starve."

"We ain't gonna starve." Sylvie stood up and gestured to the bundle. "It was nice of you to steal the bread and jam. But I can't take that."

Sylvie walked away in her threadbare pants, arms wrapped around her middle for warmth, head held high.

\*\*\*

It happened a few weeks into the New Year. The townspeople claimed that they could hear the anguished cries coming from the Gold cabin in the wee hours of the morning; the hours of the night right before sunrise when it is the darkest and coldest. Of course, this is country folklore and gossip. No one would have been able to hear a sound. They wouldn't have heard the cries of a mother in labor. They wouldn't have been privy to whether or not Gavin Gold had been so mortified at the site of his son that he snuffed the life out of him. There is no way they could have known how desperately Sylvia had clung to her mother's weakening hand, urging her to push, begging her to stay with them.

Sylvie later recounted the circumstances of that night to Harold, years after the incident. She told him that after an exhaustive labor, Laurel Gold lay in the sweat and blood soaked bed, lifeless and gone. The baby boy had been born into the world silent. Sylvie and her dad had delivered him, but it was clear from the beginning that the baby was wrong.

"Mongoloid," Gavin had whispered or maybe it was *monster*. Sylvie couldn't remember. She only knew that she had to preserve a moment with this little baby, who had for a brief second been her brother. She held him in her arms, kissed his head, and rocked him as her mother would have.

For what seemed like hours Sylvie had held onto the baby, while her mother lay on the death bed and her father slumped against the wall with his head in his hands. Eventually, they buried the baby together. He was never given a name. He was buried in her mother's arms on the cabin's property. In one night two lives disappeared. One had no record of death; the other no record of life.

Sylvie only recounted this tale one time in her life then never spoke of it again.

## Chapter 3 – Charlotte
### *Present Day*

Morning came quietly. The sky was somewhat overcast, a few ominous clouds threatening to break away from the pack, but never a rumble of thunder. The only sound was the hum of the air conditioner, one of the few upgrades made to the house over the years. For the most part we ate our breakfast silently. I was too nervous about the meaning of that cryptic note that was so out of character for my mother.

"Looks like someone left us a big, sweet mess," Nick said over the silence. I glanced in the direction he was looking to find a mound of dishes in the sink from last night. *Ants, Charlotte,* I could hear Mom's voice saying. *Once they're in you can't get them out.*

I got up to start dealing with the mess. Nick wiped his mouth and jumped up from the table. "Let me."

I shook my head, gingerly placing a hand on his upper arm. "Staying busy helps."

Dishes had to be done by hand because Mom had forever refused a dishwasher. After I left Marion for a completely different existence in Chicago, I thought it was my duty to question her about her old-fashioned ways, including her insistence to stay in the farmhouse.

"You should move your practice into the city," I had naively suggested over the phone while painting my toes a color called, ironically, My Big Sweet Mess; a rosy pink color that reminded me a of Valentine's cake.

"Why would I want to do that?" she had asked. I had called her at work. She was probably sitting in that cramped office, her white coat crumpled, a half-eaten Danish sitting on a stack of files. I felt a stab of regret for leaving her all alone.

"There would be so many more people to help."

"I have plenty of women to help here, too. In fact, looks like it's going to be a big birthing season this Christmas. A lot of ladies in town are expecting. If I left who would birth their babies? Postmaster Martin?"

I rolled my eyes as she laughed at her joke. "Why do you say it like that? Birthing? Sounds like you haven't made it past the 1950s. And, Mom, they would find someone."

Mom laughed. "All's well here, Charlotte. Don't worry about me. How are you?"

I shrugged and continued to paint my toenails.

"Charlotte, you have to use words when you speak on the telephone."

"I'm fine."

Mom sighed. Again, I could imagine what she was doing at the moment – squeezing the bridge of her nose with her thumb and forefinger. It was her *Charlotte, you make it so difficult*, gesture. "Fine is not a feeling. It's a deflection."

"I'm pretty sure fine is a feeling; at least according to Webster's Dictionary and your medical books."

"Are you visiting with Dr. Kramer? She came highly recommended."

I grunted.

"Charlotte, you are so far away. I need to know you're alright."

"Totally great, Mom. Don't worry."

Of course, she did. And of course, I wasn't fine. But sometimes you just have to pretend until it becomes the truth.

\*\*\*

At 8:30 am Nick and I pulled into the St. Mary's parking garage, parking in the spot reserved for Dr. Sylvie Day. Although it was a Monday morning the garage was still quite empty. A few cars slowly cruised by, a car door slammed here and there, but for the most part it seemed as if the garage was having a hard time waking up to the reality of a new work week. I was trying to wake up to the reality of not having a mom.

In 2000, Mom had finally relented and moved her practice from Main Street into the growing suburbs of Marion. She had little choice in the matter, quite frankly. In order to make way for overpasses and roundabouts, several roads around her Main Street office were forced to close or access was severely limited. Getting a patient to St. Mary's in a rush if something went wrong during a visit would be impossible. Always willing to sacrifice for her patients, Sylvie relocated her practice 10 miles to the north.

I had helped her pack up her files and had just loaded the last set of boxes in the backseat of my Ford Escort when I found her sitting in her waiting room, taking in the emptiness. In 2000, my mom was 66 years old. Most women her age are considering retiring, joining the Purple Hat Society, or heading out for a whirlwind world tour, but not my mom. Not Sylvie Day. She was still a force to be reckoned with, which is why it made my heart hurt and break into a million pieces watching her sit in that waiting room – her waiting room for the past 34 years – looking as lost as an Alzheimer's patient.

I sat down next to her and took her hand.

"It's so empty."

I didn't quite know what to say. So, I stayed silent waiting for her to finish. She never did. Instead, she squeezed my hand, stood up, and let it go. "Well, no use cryin' over something that you can't change. Time for a new adventure."

\*\*\*

Nick and I walked into the main lobby of the medical center. A young receptionist with long, wavy, platinum blond hair accented by lavender, pink, and cotton candy blue smiled wide at us. "Can I help you?"

I had the key to Mom's office in my right hand, the dull serrated edge pressing tightly against my palm. I hadn't realized I was holding it so tight. Or maybe I had. Did it matter? I shook my head and walked past her towards the long hallways that led to the elevators that would take me to the offices of Dr. Sylvie Day. A couple doctors walked past us, two in surgical masks, their features hidden except for their eyes and the wrinkles that feathered out from the sides. One doctor held a tall Starbucks cup, which I caught a whiff of as he walked past. He looked young, but weary – the dark purple bags were a striking contrast against his olive skin and vibrant green eyes. I wondered how much he slept. Funny thing was I couldn't remember my mother appearing this haggard, but then again there would be days when she didn't come home. Those were the days I was entrusted to my grandparents. Those were the days that my mother probably looked like death.

We rode the elevator in silence. I watched the numbers light up G – 1 – 2 – 3. Ding! The doors exhaled and opened. I turned right and knew that it would take exactly 25 steps to reach the office door. I had a thing with numbers. It was mental and I counted a lot to relieve stress. It was a technique I had learned in college. Sometimes it worked, but not always. By now I was purposely digging the key into my palm.

Nick breathed into my ear. "We can reschedule."

I released my grip on the key and shook my head. "No. Let's get this over with."

In 25 steps, I reached the door to Suite 305. The key slid into the keyhole, opening the door without any resistance. When I opened the door to the waiting room I felt a rush of panic. Instantly, I began counting the chairs in the room. 1, 2, 3, 4 . . . 15. There were 15 chairs lined along the walls as well as in the middle of the room. Of course, I already knew there would be 15. Hadn't I counted these chairs before?

The waiting room was like any other waiting room. The walls

weren't painted, but were personalized with impersonal wallpaper that could be found in a million other waiting rooms from here to the moon and back. In the left hand corner behind the door there was a magazine rack with the latest issues of *Parenthood*, *Modern Mom*, and a collection of *AARP* magazines. When I came home the summer between undergraduate and grad school, I spent a few hours a day helping mom in this office. By that point she wasn't working full days anymore. She had a younger associate, a woman named Dr. Susan Toakes who oversaw a good majority of her practice. However, on the days that she came in that summer I went with her to sort files, answer phones, and put labels on pee samples. I also made fun of the *AARP* magazines.

"Really, Mom? I think you need some new reading material."

I handed her a copy that proudly announced the *Joys of Sex after 80*. Mom had been sitting at her desk with the reading lamp on, her glasses hanging off the tip of her nose and her gray hair messily pulled up in a bun. She looked over her glasses as I handed her the magazine. "Your point, Charlotte?"

"This magazine is way too old to be in your office. You need to appeal to the younger crowd."

Mom had sat back in her chair and taken off her glasses. She chuckled at me, amused at my suggestion. "Quite frankly my patients are getting younger and younger every day. I would prefer not to market to the younger crowd. That is what condom manufacturers should be doing."

"You know what I mean. Women having babies want something to read that is informative, not comical."

"It isn't just young women that walk through my door, Charlotte. I treat women of all ages who have concerns. Someday you will understand. In fact, I have an appointment later today with Isabel Klein."

I narrowed my eyes. This was interesting. "Why?"

Mom tilted her head, giving me a quizzical look. "Why not?"

I shrugged. "Well, the last time I remember you having

anything to do with the Kleins, you were threatening bodily harm and I think that's against the Hippocratic Oath."

Mom put her glasses back on; a signal that the conversation would be ending. "My issues with Mr. Klein have no reflection on his wife. Now, kindly put the AARP magazine back unless you feel the need to learn about the pleasures of old people sex."

Now, all these years later, the AARP magazines were still there. I found it funny how little these waiting rooms changed. I had the urge to check the dates, but instead I opened the door between the waiting room and the exam rooms. At Mom's visitation Dr. Toakes told me the offices would remain closed for the remainder of the week. "Nobody really wants to come back just yet. Our inattention would be a disservice to our patients," she had said. Yet in spite of its vacancy, the office still clung to the familiar odors of antiseptic, latex, and a lingering smell of coffee.

The back offices consisted of four distinct areas. There was the records and appointment area where prescriptions were written, appointments made, and phone calls answered. This was the hub most days. From this area there were three hallways that stretched out away from the hub forming a letter E. The first hallway consisted of exam rooms. This was Mom's hallway. Her office was at the end and the exam rooms were where she would see her patients. The next hallway was the "maintenance hallway" as Mom had called it. Medical supplies were stored here, several computers containing record information were stationed at a desk, two scales were positioned at opposite ends of the hallway, and a bathroom was available for women to pee on sticks and fill plastic cups. The last hallway belonged to Dr. Toakes and was almost identical to Mom's area of the practice.

Mom's hallway seemed too quiet. I knew that she hadn't actively been practicing for the past several years, but she held office hours and consulted with patients. She had begun to leave the actual practice of delivering to Dr. Toakes. Around the age of 70, she said her hands were beginning to shake too much. "I don't trust myself anymore," she had said. I could tell this pained her, but she wouldn't risk harming a patient or a new baby.

"Wow!" Nick exclaimed. He was standing at the beginning of the hallway staring in awe at massive amount of Christmas cards that littered the wall. "Did your mom deliver all of these babies?"

I couldn't help but laugh. "Probably."

I joined him and saw that they weren't just Christmas cards, but high school graduation announcements, invitations to college graduations, and thank you letters from parents and even grandparents. The sentiments were endless.

"This is truly amazing," Nick exclaimed.

As I walked along the hallway examining the pictures, I rested my hand on my stomach. It was a small bump, hardly noticeable to anyone except me. My pants were becoming tighter as the days progressed and I had started using a rubber band looped around the button to give me a few more inches. I wasn't too excited about buying those elasticized maternity pants.

"I just wish I had told her," I lamented. "She would have been so excited."

"Charlie, you didn't want to worry her. I am sure she knows and is up there ready to protect you and our baby."

I nodded in agreement, but it didn't make the remorse go away. There were a million reasons why I hadn't told Mom about this pregnancy, but Nick was right. I didn't want to worry her. At 36 years old, I had been well on my way to being an "older" parent, as my mom was when she had me. It wasn't that Nick and I hadn't tried to get pregnant. In fact, we tried all the time. So much that the fun of making a baby had started to wane and it became more like a job.

We got pregnant three times, but each time there was a reason that the pregnancy wasn't viable. The first pregnancy I miscarried just before 10 weeks. The truth was I hadn't even known I was pregnant, not really. We had just started trying and I figured it would take a while. The second pregnancy failed again around 10 weeks. This time it was an ectopic pregnancy. My OB had suggested I medically abort the fetus instead of opting for surgery, but in the end the medicine didn't work and I had to have surgery to prevent my left fallopian tube from rupturing. The scarring left me with one sustainable tube. Mom had been livid that my doctor had taken the whole matter so lightly.

The third pregnancy left a whole in my heart; in my entire existence. I made it to five months. I had sonograms hanging on the stainless steel refrigerator in our apartment. Nick and I had decided that our gorgeous apartment overlooking Lincoln Park was perfect for a couple, but lacked the warmth that a new baby needed. We started looking for homes near Gurnee where the neighborhoods were inviting for families with small children. I had even begun placing orders for sturdy, rough and tumble, masculine furniture from Pottery Barn. I had a box that was overflowing with clothing in blues, browns, and reds. I had always insisted that I would approach motherhood in a modern fashion, throwing aside all stereotypes. But when the obstetrician told me a little boy was floating around in my womb, I found myself unable to be deterred from the blue onesies and the brown sweaters with little puppies on them that made no sense for a newborn, but I needed them nonetheless. Then October 1, 2010 happened.

Nick was out of town in Milwaukee at a young lawyers' convention. I had been at my office on North State Street for twelve hours straight dealing with clients who didn't know the difference between multi-level advertising and putting flyers on cars when the first pains seized my abdomen. It was a searing pain that seemed to wrap itself around me and squeeze unrelentingly. The pain was worse than what I had experienced with the ectopic. I tried to sit down, convinced the problem was overexertion and the pain would go away if I just relaxed for a bit. Then I felt a release between my legs and a horrifying gush of blood spilled forth, soaking the chair and the floor beneath my feet. I screamed. My co-worker and friend, Amy, who had been a bridesmaid at my wedding and who was secretly planning a baby shower for me, heard the blood-curdling scream and found me unconscious.

It was Mom who I found sitting at my bedside in the hospital when I woke. She held my hand, stroking it softly. "It's not a punishment. It just is what it is," were the words she spoke when I opened my eyes. Apparently, I had been rambling while I was unconscious. At the time I ignored her words, turned my head, and buried my face in the pillow. I could already feel the hollowness in my womb. I knew he was gone.

With the drama and disappointment of the previous three pregnancies, I hadn't wanted to worry her with the newness of this pregnancy. I also hadn't wanted to disappoint her. I could tell that she was hoping I would consider other means of having children instead of continuously risking my own well-being. My own doctor had begun to have those discussions with me as well and I knew that if this pregnancy didn't succeed, it would be the last time I carried a biological child inside of me. But I had a feeling this pregnancy would be different. There wasn't any other choice.

The door to the waiting room opened, interrupting my thoughts. I heard the distinctive smack of a cane against the door and labored breathing as the intruder struggled to push the heavy door open. By the time Nick and I made it to the waiting room, Harold Klein was standing against the door wiping his forehead with the back of his hand, a few wisps of what was left of his hair sticking straight up. He attempted a halfway smile, but for a man unaccustomed to smiling the gesture came off awkward.

"Isabel told me to stop smoking those Pall Malls and, in her words, nasty cigars. Guess I should have taken her advice sooner."

"Are you alright?" I asked.

He nodded the way old men do, dismissively, and I could tell he was slightly embarrassed to be caught in a moment of frailty. "Yes, yes. Just give me a moment to catch my breath." He sat down in one of the chairs, resting his hands on his knees with his back hunched over.

Nick and I stood uncomfortably together as Harold struggled

to regain his composure. Finally, after what seemed like twenty minutes, he pushed off his knees with his hands, straightened his back, dug his cane into the blue speckled carpet, and stood up. He signaled that we should follow him.

He headed to the door that separated the waiting room from the exam area. Nick jumped ahead of him and grabbed the door, looking back at me and winking as he easily opened the door. I stifled a giggle.

Harold didn't let this gesture go unnoticed. "Yes, yes. Show those muscles, young man. Show them off while you can because eventually they will go limp and be as useful as wet noodles."

Nick looked at me in dismay at Harold's rudeness. I simply shrugged. His brusque manners didn't surprise me. I had witnessed enough interactions between him and my mom over the years to understand that his personality was the kind that made people squirm and keep looking at their watches, counting down the minutes until their encounter would be over.

When we reached my mom's office, Harold motioned for us to take a seat in the two chairs that were in front of her massive desk. At just barely five feet tall, she had looked like a pygmy sitting behind this desk. Harold reached into the lapel of his sports coat and withdrew a pair of reading glasses. "Your eyes go too, young man, remember that."

Again there was a disturbing silence. Silences bugged me. If I couldn't fill them with conversation then I would turn on music, start humming, or revert back to an annoying teenage habit that involved popping my knuckles. "Not to rush you," I said. "But the curiosity is too much for me to bear much longer. Why did you ask us to meet you here? Is it about my mom's will? Does Dr. Toakes need me to sign something to release Mom's share of the practice to her?"

"Why would you think this is about your mother's will?"

"I assumed you were her lawyer?"

Harold laughed. "Hardly. I haven't practiced law in years. Truth be told, I haven't done much of anything, really. Not since. . .

well, that doesn't matter. No, no. I am here for an entirely different reason."

I felt a sense of dread and anxiousness start to build in my chest. The feeling always came on slowly, but would quickly begin to spread and reverberate throughout my body. *It feels like butterfly wings flapping wildly in my chest*, I had told that shrink Mom had sent me to during my first year of college. She had taught me methods for dealing with this symptom of anxiety and, like most shrinks, eventually gave me pills.

I hadn't needed those medicinal remedies for years, but now I was wishing I had them. Instead, I gripped the key again, letting it calm and soothe me by inducing just a small bit of pain. I knew I would be disappointing my mom right now if she knew I was reverting back to old methods of dealing with anxious moments, but I couldn't help myself. We – the three of us – were teetering on the cusp of something bad; something life changing. I could feel it. The butterflies were beginning to flutter out of control.

"Then what is this all about? Tell me."

Nick put his hand on my knee, which by now was rapidly bouncing up and down. "Calm down, Charlotte."

Harold looked over his glasses at me and then addressed Nick. "What's going on? Does she have seizures?"

"What?" Nick asked.

"Seizures. You know? Those tics that people get where they start bouncing all over the floor."

"What would ever make you ask me a question like that?"

Harold pointed to me. "Because her face is red, her body is shaking, and I'm not comfortable with this situation."

Nick continued to rub my knee in a rhythmic and soothing circular motion, calming me down slowly with his touch. "I think she's been through quite a lot these past several days. It's nerves."

"Maybe we should do this a different day." Harold suggested.

"No," I said firmly. "What was that letter all about that you gave me yesterday? That's what this has to do with, no?"

"When Sylvie found out she was sick she gave me that letter to give to you when the time was right."

"Right for what?"

"I guess she meant when she died."

"When did she give you that letter?"

"About seven months ago."

I was stunned into silence. The cancer that had invaded my mother's brain was aggressive. At least that is what the doctors told me when I rushed to the hospital – this hospital – late last week when Mom was admitted. It was likely that she hadn't been taking care of herself, ignored some obvious symptoms, and by the time the diagnosis was made it had been too late. She had already fallen into a coma.

But if what Harold was saying was true then there had been time; time to talk and make amends for silly stuff, such as forgetting to call her every Sunday like I promised. Or for the bigger stuff that had gone unspoken between us for so many years. Why had she kept this illness from me?

As if reading my thoughts, Harold continued. "Sylvie was a tough person to know. Who knows why she did some of the things she did. I knew that she hadn't told you about her cancer when she gave me this note and she made it quite clear that I was not to make contact with you until after her death. Goddamn, your mother was so stubborn. It was a flaw."

I glared at Harold. Who was he to speak about my mother like this? "Well, she didn't think too kindly of you either, Mr. Klein."

Harold guffawed. "Ha! My dear, you do not have to remind me about your mother's loathing towards me. I put up with that for way too many years, but she had her reasons. Although she managed to bury her animosities when I needed her help with Isabel. But that is neither here nor there."

He pushed his chair back and walked over to a large Ansel Adams print that hung on Mom's wall. It was an all-purpose picture of the sun setting over the ocean that could have been just as useful in a hair salon, college dorm room, or sperm donor's clinic. Nothing special; it had been part of a bargain bin that had been set out on the street by Mrs. Fuller, owner of the Mary Martha Thrift Shop that was next to Mom's Main Street practice.

Harold removed the picture, revealing a small safe that had been built into the wall. He started to turn the dial, but paused. "What's your birthday, again?"

On auto-pilot I answered without hesitation. "February 8, 1975."

He nodded and turned the safe's dial tenderly, carefully. When he rotated to the final number, the safe door popped open. He reached inside and brought out a manila file that looked no different than the files Mom kept in her office.

He sat back down, readjusting his glasses. "You asked about the legalities of your mother's will, yes? Your mother's will is in this file. The executor of the will is listed and you can contact them to move forward. However, there may be some bumps in the road."

"I don't understand." This was it. This was the cliff. We were about ready to jump off together. I reached for Nick's hand.

"You see, your mother wasn't an angel, Charlotte. She may have been the treasure of this town, but there are things you don't know about her. She may have rose high on her pedestal, but she was human like the rest of us with flaws and secrets."

"Whatever you are trying to say, just say it."

"You weren't her first child. You weren't her only child. She had another daughter, Charlotte. One she kept from you and one she kept from me."

Chapter 4 – Harold
*1953*

During the summer of 1953 Harold was only interested in two things: his 1953 Dodge B-series pickup and baseball. The truck was a graduation gift from his parents; an excessive extravagance compared to the gifts of watches and Zenith tube radios that his friends had received. However, whatever guilt he harbored (which wasn't much in all honesty) about receiving such an overstated gift didn't last beyond the moment he slid behind the wheel and turned the ignition. When the engine began to whirr and the steering wheel vibrate underneath his hands, Harold would close his eyes, a ridiculous grin spread across his face, and he would put the car in drive, and take off at a reckless speed down Main Street and out onto the back roads.

Police Chief Mac Donaldson, Marion's one and only law enforcement officer (therefore, the title meant nothing to Harold or anyone else for that matter) had issued Harold warnings on many occasions for his excessive speed.

"You'd think he was gearing up to compete for a spot on the World Sportscar Championship circuit," Donaldson told Harold's dad one day.

His dad laughed. "It's a truck, not an Aston Martin DB3."

"Still," Donaldson insisted. "He needs to be more careful. He could hurt himself or someone else. I done chased him across that Payne Bridge more than once. He doesn't seem to care."

The Payne Bridge, referred to as the *pain bridge* by locals, was a one-lane bridge that stretched about one hundred yards over Bare Bottom Creek. Daredevils liked to race across the bridge playing chicken with suspecting and unsuspecting cars. It was the site of more than one deadly accident.

"I'll talk to him," the elder Klein had conceded.

Donaldson tipped his hat. "I would appreciate that very much. And maybe tell him to stop honkin' that horn so much and keep his head in the cab. That hootin' and hollerin' he is doing through town is starting to earn him a reputation as a pompous jackass."

The last thing Harold cared about was his reputation, at least not in a town as inconsequential as this one. He had bigger plans on the horizon that would take him far away from the landlocked farms and the incessant gossip that sprinkled from the wings of the social butterflies that overpopulated this place.

In 1953, at the age of 18, Harold was going to be a major league ball player. Okay, well maybe that was overstating the situation. But, if anyone assumed or was led to believe this was the situation, Harold would not have corrected them. No one ever asked, though, and that was fine with Harold. He was perfectly content with keeping this his little secret.

***

Kent Baker was a large man that oozed excess. His button down shirt pulled against his chest, the buttons straining and threatening to pop, while his stomach swung over his belt. When he sat at the Klein's kitchen table he lowered himself slowly into the chair, exhaling loudly as if the act of sitting was exhausting. What struck Harold most about this man was his face. It was quite thin and didn't match his body at all. It was as if someone had removed the head of the original owner of the body and replaced it.

All through dinner the man kept staring at Harold, which was making him grow increasingly alarmed. His whole life he had been warned about strange men that liked to corner boys and make them do illicit things like touching and rubbing. He wondered if Kent Baker was one of these men.

"Where's your appetite, boy?" Baker asked as he pushed a piece of bread into his mouth. Crumbs and spittle fell from the sides of his mouth.

Harold pushed the spaghetti around on his plate. It was a fancy meal that wasn't usually on the dinner menu in a household that preferred meat and potatoes. His palette wasn't used to the mushiness, the odd flavors of the sauce, and the fact that it was meatless. A meal without meat didn't make sense. Actually it made Harold quite nauseated and sitting at this table with a man who probably wanted to touch his balls didn't make it any better.

The meal continued for another thirty minutes with Baker asking for seconds and thirds. Harold's mother would jump up immediately to oblige, while his father sat there smiling like a goon. *What is wrong with my parents,* Harold thought. They were putting on airs and acting like ass-kissers without brains.

The only person at the table that was acting even remotely in her same, everyday manner was Mabel. She poked at her noodles, cutting them into tiny pieces that she could scoop up with a spoon. Every few seconds she would sigh and twirl her hair, glancing at the clock on the wall. It was a Friday night, which meant she had a date with Ed Hardy, her current beau. Mabel had so many suitors that Harold couldn't keep up with them. He couldn't quite see why boys were even attracted to her. She may have been considered pretty, but she was bossy and snobbish. Who could possibly find that attractive?

"Mother, when is dinner going to be finished? Ed will be here any moment and I still haven't fixed my hair properly."

Their mother glared at her. "Don't be rude. Dinner will be finished when our guest is through enjoying his meal. If Ed arrives he is welcome to join us."

Mabel rolled her eyes, sat back, crossed her arms, and pouted. Turns out Ed never showed up that night. He actually dumped her for Sally Harkins the next day, which would have been enough to make Harold ecstatic if his life hadn't changed about ten minutes later.

It turns out that Kent Baker wasn't a child molester and he wasn't just a friendly associate of his father's. Baker was a bona fide ball scout. He had been passing through town and stopped in to say hello to his old college buddy, Harold Klein Sr. One thing led to another and here they were, sitting on the front porch where they had moved after Harold's mother had shooed them out of the kitchen.

"Your old man here tells me you like to toss the ball," Baker said when they had retired to the front porch after dinner.

Harold shrugged. "Yes, sir. That's true. You play?"

Baker's laugh rumbled through the ground like an earthquake rolling along landscape. His stomach bounced up and down and his cheeks flushed. "Now that's funny, son."

Harold didn't know how to react to people, so he stayed mute. Aside from his parents and Mabel, he was generally awkward around others. Gauging social cues was difficult for him, which is why he stuck with what he knew best – tossing the ball.

"What position you play?"

"Anything."

Baker raised his eyes and looked over at his Harold Sr. "He says anything."

Harold Sr. opened his palms and raised them to the sky. "Not much competition or interest in baseball out here. You get put wherever. Not much strategy involved."

"You boys winning any titles?"

Harold leaned against the rail of the porch, his hands in his back pockets. "Like Pops said, ain't much strategy so we aren't winning much. Who wants to play against a bunch of country folk anyway? Half the guys don't even show up to the games when it's birthing season on the farm."

Baker considered this. He looked Harold over. His eyes narrowed, becoming even smaller on his already unusually small head. "There isn't much to you, boy. My ball players have a little more muscle."

Harold knew he was scrawny, but he certainly didn't appreciate this behemoth man commenting on his lack of athletic physique. He tried to put on weight and muscle, but he wasn't raised to do manual labor like other boys in the town. His father was a lawyer for Christ's sake. Lifting a finger or shucking corn wasn't really part of their lifestyle.

Baker rubbed his stubble in a manner that seemed planned, yet subconscious. "Suppose it makes you fast. You good at stealing bases?"

"They're pretty easy to take, sir."

Baker slapped at a bug on his wrist. The button on his pants had popped open. It was quite disgraceful. Harold looked down at his shoes to avoid staring at the man's shortcomings.

"Nice to see your father raised a polite boy, but put those 'sirs' away. My boys call me Baker. You call me that, too."

Harold nodded and silence followed. The only sound that could be detected for what seemed like forever was the clanging of dishes in the kitchen and the sound of Mabel's heels clicking against the linoleum as she paced back and forth waiting for Ed to show.

"Let's toss the ball tomorrow; you and your father. Let me get a look at you and we'll talk." Baker stood. Shook hands with Harold Sr. and then nodded at Harold. "Looking forward to seeing what you got."

That night Harold didn't sleep. He didn't have anything to measure the feasibility of this situation against. He had heard of ball players like Babe Ruth (could he even be forward enough to believe he was as special as The Babe?) being plucked out of thin air and brought on to play in the big leagues, but that didn't happen to regular people did it? Not people like Harold, who didn't have a social bone in his body; who was more comfortable in solitude than being in the approved social graces of others.

Baker arrived early the next morning, but Harold's performance was clumsy. It felt strange to toss the ball in the backyard with his father, presumably trying out for a new life far away from this confined community. It wasn't like playing a real game where his skills could be adequately gauged and assessed. Harold Sr. had a hard time catching the ball, which made Harold's throwing skills look laughable. Batting was about the same. He only got a few decent hits off the old man's pitching. This too was laughable. And stealing? How could he demonstrate his litheness and timing when there wasn't anyone around to challenge him? When Baker finally motioned for them to stop, Harold felt utterly defeated.

"Here's the problem I have," Baker stated when the three men had resumed their positions on the porch. Baker, sitting in a chair this time with his pants securely fastened, his father perched on the edge of his, his left toes thumping against the floor (something he only did when he was nervous, Harold knew), and Harold leaning against the railing, waiting to be delivered the blow. "I suppose you heard the rumors. The Browns are considering a move out to the East Coast. Baltimore is looking to be their new home base. But here's the problem. They want to reinvent the team. They don't want the same old Midwest blood soaking the hopes, dreams, and prospects of a bigger and better East Coast team. Hell, they're even thinking of changing the name. Some sort of bird, I think."

Baker took a sip of water. "I'm afraid some of my boys – good fellas they are and damn good ball players – are going to be looking for new teams. Makes me damn furious, but that's the business and I have to go where the team goes. This means I need some new prospects. The ball season is already in full swing and we don't need players now, but I will need them next year. Here's what I can offer you. It's a chance to play real ball and hone your skills. Right now they're rough. Of course, you may do better when you get better teammates. No offense, Klein."

Harold's father chuckled. His foot had stopped tapping. He was starting to relax. "None taken, Kent. I never claimed to be talented at anything other than standing in front of a judge."

"I'm willing to take you on as a personal project and favor to your father."

"Like a charity case?" Harold asked.

"Harold," his father said. The tone was cautionary, but Baker held up his hand to discourage any farther scolding.

"I am not an altruistic person. Actually, I am quite selfish and only interested in how most situations benefit me. When I find talent and my talent proves they are worthy I get rewarded generously. So do not underestimate or insult me by taking that tone. You are being offered a chance to live out your dream in a way that most boys from shithole, trivial places like this don't often get a chance to. Now, you are more than welcome to misunderstand the offer I am making to you and make a choice to continue to bale hay and wrestle with pigs. Or, you can listen to my offer and make a wiser decision."

Harold had never really been put in his place before by an adult other than his father. He was usually coddled and handfed by people who only bothered to talk to him because of his father's elevated status in the community. This was new territory for Harold and while he felt shame he also felt a fire stirring in his belly – excitement after years of boredom. "I'm listening."

"You will travel with the team this summer. Take batting practice and work on your fielding. You will also help out in the clubhouse, taking care of things such as washing clothing, cleaning bats, counting balls, and other matters that seem to have nothing to do with playing ball but will make you appreciate being on the field when the time comes."

"You want me to pack my bags tonight?"

"You can join the team at the end of July. We'll be headed back this way for a few games and you can tag along then. Won't be much of a season, but your father expects you to graduate with your class and I agree. The lifespan of a ball player is affected by many, many factors that are out of one's control. To not graduate high school would be irresponsible. The road will be there in July."

The remainder of the days between then and graduation had been unbearable. The boredom and the excitement were hard to contain. Harold would have sold his soul to be allowed to fast forward to his new life. Instead he was forced to wait for his new life to begin. Now that he had his new truck that meant spending countless hours speeding down the back roads of Marion, watching the dust plume behind him, and celebrating his impending release from the cornfield prison.

\*\*\*

As excited as he was to get on the road with Baker, the truth was that baseball wasn't the only thing on Harold's mind that summer. He had spent most of April and May ignoring much else in his life, except for Sylvie. After her mother had passed away years earlier, she had slowly faded from his life. The friendship between Sylvie and his sister had waned as Mabel became more pampered and Sylvie more hardboiled. It seemed their lives had separated as quickly as oil and water separate when mixed together.

That isn't to say that she and Mabel didn't still get along. Sometimes Sylvie would emerge from the thickness of the forest and meet his sister on those infamous porch steps where Sylvie had once chastised him for his wickedness, but she no longer carried that rag doll with her and her appearance had changed, too. She still wore threadbare clothes and shoes with damaged soles that flapped steadily underneath her feet as she walked, keeping a silent rhythm when she padded across the grass. Harold would watch Sylvie and Mabel from his bedroom window as they talked. Although most times it seemed as if neither had much to say; at 18, having led very different lives, neither could relate to the other one's situation. Children know how to put aside their differences, while adults – even newly formed adults – let these differences define them.

But for reasons he didn't really understand, Sylvie continued to fascinate Harold. She rarely spoke to anyone, even in school. She kept her head down, her long, unkempt wavy hair falling into her face as her pencil glided across the paper. When school let out she didn't head over to Millie's Tavern for root beer floats and idle chatter like her classmates. Instead she worked a job helping out Carnie Eden, the only other person in town crazier than Gavin Gold. Most people considered her blasphemous and a witch and in a town like Marion, they were basically the same thing.

Old lady Eden lived in a tiny cottage nestled between the courthouse and the post office. It seemed like an odd place to have a home, but rural towns sprouted up in the oddest places and some folks just refused to budge to make room for progress. The cottage invited a lot of antics and pranks from local kids, especially at Halloween time. This was when the cruelty of children (and quite possible some adults) was at its worse. One Halloween when Harold was still participating in acts of torture with Bart Cullins, they had nabbed a stray black cat (or at least that's what Harold had made himself believe, even though he knew the cat belonged to one of the Foster boys), sliced it open, and left it on her front porch. The next day the cat was gone, except for its tail. Harold and Bart made up stories about seeing old lady Eden use the cat in a simmering stew that she consumed to make her powers stronger.

The truth was that Eden had a memory disease. She could remember the first time she saw a Negro walking into Marion, ratty and dirty from walking for days out of the South to what he thought would be a better existence past the Mason-Dixon Line. She could remember the way that her husband, dead for over 40 years, had touched her on their wedding night and the way her body responded like a million fire ants were jumping across her skin. But she couldn't remember her name or why such a strange young girl kept coming to her house every day when the sun had started to fall from the sky.

Old lady Eden's cottage was directly across the street from Harold's father's law office and since Harold was regularly forced to help out his dad in the office, he had plenty of opportunities to spy on Sylvie. It made absolutely no sense to Harold why he had become so fascinated with her. It started years earlier and had dissipated at times, but when those weird butterfly sensations found their way into his gut again they were always stronger than the last time.

Sylvie moved in and out of the cottage; sweeping the threshold, washing the windows, and hanging laundry. She kept her face shielded with her long hair, just as she did in school. Even as spring progressed and temperatures rose far past comfortable, she never pulled it back. Harold thought it was beautiful, regardless of how unkempt it was. When the sunlight bounced off her tresses it looked like she wore a hallo of gold. Harold caught himself wondering what it would feel like to touch her hair, entwine his fingers in it. These thoughts were no good, Harold always reminded himself. He had plans and they weren't to get involved with a crazy man's daughter.

When Laurel Gold passed after giving birth to a dead baby years earlier, whatever sanity Gavin Gold had managed to cling to left him quickly. He had spent too many nights and twice as many days sitting in the corner of Millie's Tavern nursing drinks – and they weren't root beer. When his tab eventually got higher than his tolerance level, he resorted to skimming whiskey from an unsavory crowd that hung out by the railroad tracks.

If Gavin Gold knew what a joke he was to the rest of Marion, he certainly gave no notion of caring. When he wasn't stumbling along the railroad tracks with a cheap bottle of bourbon in his hands, you could find him crouched in the alleys between area businesses, sleeping off his latest binge. Often Sylvie would come gather him and walk with him back home through the dense forest that separated his kind from townies, both of them stumbling together – him from the alcohol and her from his dead weight leaning against her thin frame.

"If you want something, just ask," Sylvie had said one afternoon in mid-April.

Harold jumped at the sound of her voice. He hadn't heard it in years and he hadn't noticed her walk across the street with that broom in her hand and an angry scowl on her face.

"I'm getting damn near tired of being spied on. What is it you want, Harold?"

He studied her. This was the first time she had been up close to him in years. It was also the first time he saw her face, unshielded by her hair. *God*, he thought, *she is an angel.* Everything about her was perfect, from her symmetrical eyes to her pink, ripe lips. Those butterflies started fluttering again, only this time his heart raced and his lower region began to come alive. He turned away from her so she wouldn't notice his desire and his humanness.

"Not sure why you think you're so noticeable," he said. He tried to ignore her and make the odd sensations in his body go away, but true to her nature she wouldn't leave well enough alone. She grabbed his shoulder and spun him around. For such an emaciated creature she was quite strong.

"What no good are you up to? You better not be planning a cruel joke on Miss Eden. She is a kind, gentle woman who has done no one any harm. I just don't understand the meanness of people. "

"I'm not interested in old lady Eden."

"Then why are you watching me every day?"

How could he answer that question when he didn't know the answer himself? Instead of answering her question, he surprised himself by eliciting concern. "How are you?"

"What?" she asked.

"How are you?" he said again.

Sylvie looked at him, befuddled. He couldn't possibly know this, but no one had ever asked her how she was before. Not one time in her life had anyone ever expressed concern for Sylvie Gold, not even her own father after her mother had died.

She fiddled with the broom still in her hand, but it was lowered and not posing a threat. "I guess I'm fine. Why do you care?"

Harold shrugged. "Your hair is pretty."

She touched her hair and looked away. "What do you want?"

Harold shuffled his feet and stuck his hands in his back pockets. This was his nervous gesture. His mother was constantly mending his back pockets because of how often he tore them from shoving his hands in his pocket. "Well, you never go to Millie's after school."

"Yeah, so?"

"Well, I was just wondering why. I mean, do you want to go?"

"With you?" she asked.

"Mabel can come too, I guess, although she spends way too much time with Mary Clark trying to get the attention of her older brother. It's pathetic." He offered a self-conscious smile. Smiling was something he wasn't accustomed to.

Sylvie glanced towards old lady Eden's cottage, "Yeah, I don't know."

"You don't have to pay."

"I should."

"But you don't have to."

Sylvie ignored him. She chewed her bottom lip, appearing to weigh the pros and cons, while trying to determine Harold's angle. "Maybe after classes on Friday."

Harold started to smile again, but Sylvie turned away. She ran across the street to the cottage, her worn shoes flapping again loudly as they pounded across the pavement.

\*\*\*

That next Friday Sylvie and Harold sat at the bar at Millie's Tavern with about a dozen other kids who were laughing and chattering incessantly. It gave Harold a headache and Sylvie looked equally uncomfortable. Mabel had walked with the two of them to Millie's, but hadn't stayed. She pulled Sylvie aside the moment they were in the front door and told her she had to go. Mary Clark's brother had promised to pick her up in his Nash Rambler in five minutes.

"It's so exciting. I can't believe this is really happening. Usually he only drives with older girls. It's a dream come true, "she said as she grabbed Sylvie's shoulders and jumped up and down. Harold rolled his eyes and feigned vomiting when Mabel went onto say, "I hear those cars have huge backseats, if you know what I mean."

So, with Mabel gone exploring the backseat of Mary Clark's brother's Nash Rambler, it was just Harold and Sylvie sitting alone at the bar in a sea of teenage jubilance, both feeling incredibly out of place.

"Do you want to take a walk?" Harold asked.

Sylvie nodded. "Anything would be better than sitting here. This root beer tastes disgusting. Who puts ice cream in root beer?"

Harold laid two nickels on the counter and stood up to go. But Sylvie grabbed his arm and plopped his nickel into his hand before putting her own nickel besides his. "I told you long ago, I don't take charity."

They walked out onto Main Street. At this time of day it was busy with cars and crowded with people. People were generally in a good mood, excited for closing the workweek and returning home to their families for a couple days of rest. Men entered the bank, cashing their checks. The women gathered at the grocers. Harold saw his own father standing on the front porch of the law offices, talking with a client. Harold grabbed Sylvie's arm and directed her in the opposite direction.

He didn't want his father to get the wrong idea. If his father saw him he would have to explain why he was in the company of Sylvie Gold. He wasn't interested in explaining why, because this would mean he would have to admit that he didn't know. Worse than that, he would have to admit that he did know and that the reason he wanted to spend time with her was because he was lonely.

"You don't have many social graces, do you Harold Klein?"

"And you do?"

"Just because I live in a cabin in the woods without running water or electricity doesn't mean I lack manners."

"You don't have water?" Harold couldn't imagine that. "Or electricity?"

Sylvie laughed at his bewildered expression. "Coming from privilege like you do that must be hard to imagine. Why do you think I always spent all those endless days at your house? It certainly wasn't because I wanted to see your ugly face."

"Actually, I thought it was to torture me."

"Well, that too. You made it so easy."

Sylvie was wearing a pair of men's pants, which made her stand out even more from the other girls at school and in town. She put her hands in the pockets and Harold noticed that this action made the pants slip a little further off her hipbones. "We used to have electricity, when I was like five or six, but then my papa started working less and less and we couldn't afford it."

"What's it like?"

Sylvie shrugged. "You get used to it. Winter is the hardest because sometimes it gets so bitterly cold that even five quilts and a roaring fire won't warm your insides." They continued to walk towards nowhere in particular when Sylvie asked, "You know what I miss most?"

"No, what?"

"Well, it's not really what I miss because you can't miss something you never had. But what I would love to know is what it feels like to take a bath in a real tub. You know, those ones with the claw feet. It gets tiring bringing water from the creek, boiling it over the fire, and then only having enough to really just barely wet your body. But it can't be changed, so why worry about it?"

Harold nodded. "Graduation is coming up. You staying in town?"

"Where would I possibly go?"

"You seem smart. You're always concentrating on the assignments in class."

"It keeps me busy. Besides, I like school. Don't you?"

Harold chuckled. "What is there to like about school? It takes up too much time during my day when there are so many other things I could be doing."

"Like skinning cats?"

Darkness fell over Harold's face. It was shame that would quickly turn to anger if he wasn't careful. "I am not that same person."

Sylvie just nodded. She didn't apologize or acknowledge the error in her statement in any way. She simply said, "That's good, Harold, because that was wrong."

For a brief second the butterflies flew away. Maybe he was wrong about his feelings toward Sylvie. She wouldn't ever be able to see him any other way. But when he looked at her profile he realized he didn't care. He just wanted to be with her in whatever capacity was possible.

***

This is how he and Sylvie bookended their weeks; meeting on Monday and Friday afternoons at Millie's after school and sitting at the barstools, avoiding the bitter root beer floats, and actually speaking very little to each other. This pattern continued for weeks until one day Sylvie didn't show up at school or the tavern. Harold went nosing around old lady Eden's cottage, but didn't find Sylvie there either.

He squinted up at the sun, still high enough in the sky to promise a couple more hours of daylight, and headed off in the direction of the woods behind his house. He wouldn't admit it to a single soul had they asked, but those woods scared him as much now as they did when he was ten years old and had slogged through them to bring Sylvie the food she had so ungratefully thrown at his feet. Would she be grateful now that he cared enough to come searching for her, putting his own suspicions of the ghosts and real life vagrants that haunted these woods aside?

He and Sylvie had not categorized their friendship, if you could even call it that. He was old enough now to figure out that his feelings toward her were tender – maybe even love – but he was constantly questioning what Sylvie wanted out of the odd arrangement. She rarely spoke and when she did her words were either hostile or patronizing. It was as if she always wanted him to know she had the upper hand. This both angered and excited him. At the very least she was more interesting than the other girls he could have wasted his time with, but at the other end of the spectrum he felt that there was a cellular purpose that connected him to her. She may be Mabel's friend, but she was a part of their lives because she was meant to fill a void of unmistakable emptiness that Harold wasn't sure anything else in life could ever fill.

The last time he had hiked through the woods to Sylvie's cabin the ground was hard from the frosty air and the trees bare, except for the pine trees that refused to let winter strip them of their foliage. This time the ground sank underneath his feet. The branches from the lower canopy of trees smacked his face, scolding him for entering their territory. They left welts and scratches on his hands. The shade of the forest chilled him and he had wished he'd thought about bringing a jacket.

The journey through the trail-less forest continued to stretch out before him. *How did Sylvie walk through this mass of trees every day without getting lost or swallowed whole*, he thought. Her skin was free of blemishes or branch burn. Even her unkempt hair wasn't littered with leaves like his was now. The forest must have laid out the red carpet for Sylvie to let her pass unharmed and unmarred. After all, this was her home. He was the intruder.

As he came to the edge of the forest, he saw the cabin and stopped. It appeared smaller and in even worse condition than it had eight years earlier. As he stood taking it in, a sound alerted him. It was a whimper; an animal maybe. Had Gavin set a trap to catch a spring hare? It dawned on Harold at that moment that he didn't even know how Sylvie found food when she wasn't in town. On the heels of that thought, as he looked at their rundown cabin, it also occurred to him that maybe he and Sylvie didn't talk because there wasn't much to say. Sylvie didn't want to waste her efforts on him explaining that he was privileged and she was just – here. She existed, but to what capacity?

Harold walked slowly towards the sound and realized that it wasn't the whimper of a wounded animal, but the sobbing of a wounded soul. Sylvie knelt on the ground about a hundred yards from him. She wore the same ragged pants she always wore and a white sleeveless shirt that looked like it belonged to her father. She was on her knees hunched over, her hair wrapping itself around her neck like a scarf. Harold hesitated, deciding how to turn and run without being seen. Yes, he was a coward. It was to be his trademark.

He had seen women and girls cry before. Mabel cried if you looked at her the wrong way and his mother cried when she heard of close friends that were ill, but their cries were not like this. Sylvie's tears were undiluted, brimming with fresh pain and suffering. It scared Harold because it was too raw and savage. It embarrassed him and made him feel unworthy at the same time.

A squirrel rustled in the woods and the forest betrayed him, gave him away. Sylvie looked up sharply. Her eyes were daggers; mean and unforgiving. Her lower lids were red and inflamed from crying and snot dripped from her nostrils. She turned away from him, running the back of her hand underneath her nose. "What?"

"You weren't at school today," he said. What else was there to say, really, that would explain why he was here when he couldn't explain it himself?

"Go away."

"Are you alright?"

Sylvie glared at him. "That is about the most asinine question that has ever fallen from your lips. And that's saying something since you happen to say a lot of dim witted things."

"What is wrong?" Harold asked.

"Not interested, Harold. Leave. Go back to your friends and your perfect existence. You are not welcome here."

"I didn't bring charity this time."

Sylvie guffawed. "Yes, you did. Charity isn't always a gift or food. The charity that you brought is written all over your face. It's pity. I don't need charity or pity."

Harold looked around to see if anyone was watching them, or even someone who might be able to help. Either way, he didn't see a soul. He put one foot in front of the other and approached Sylvie like you would approach a wounded animal – cautiously and uncertain. "Maybe I can help."

She didn't respond, but she didn't lash out at him when he sat down next to her. Instead she sat back on her bottom and scooted away from him. He looked down at where she had been sitting and saw two rather large rocks. They must have come from the Bare Bottom Creek, but farther downstream where you could find chunks of rocks that hadn't been polished bare from feet and bottoms. The rocks had been inexpertly carved with dates, but no names. There were drawings on the rocks that looked like they had been made by a child who had gotten a hold of crayons and drawn hearts, flowers, and angel wings. This made Harold remember the time that he and Mabel had decided to trace each other's body on the kitchen floor when they were about four. It had taken his mother nearly two days of using boiling water to get up the waxy residue and it still looked like a crime scene outline when sun filtered through the kitchen window just right at midday.

Harold sat back opposite of Sylvie and only managed to utter, "Oh."

"Those rumors aren't true," she said.

"What rumors?" Harold responded.

"Don't play dumb. Everyone talks in this stupid town. All of you walk around here like you don't have shame. Everyone has shame, but the shame that my Daddy feels isn't his to own. He didn't hurt them. God hurt them."

Harold didn't know how to respond to this. So he kept quiet and Sylvie kept talking.

"My Daddy may not be the most sober of the people that walk around this godforsaken place, but he wouldn't harm a soul; at least not a soul that didn't deserve it. But now," Sylvie stopped to wipe her nose which had erupted again, "everyone has made him a pariah. A grieving man has become nothing more than a pariah, something to be laughed at and made fun of. No one killed my momma and my brother; no one real at least. If you want to blame someone for snuffing the life out of two innocent souls fine, but get your story straight."

Harold stayed an arm's length away from Sylvie as she told him the true version of that night all those years ago. He wanted to reach out and comfort her, wrap her in a warm embrace, smooth and smell her hair. He wanted to gingerly wipe the tears that dripped onto her cheeks with his finger, but he knew his advances would be unwanted. He knew that he was being allowed to be a witness to her pain, but he couldn't participate in it nor could he soothe it. He wasn't sure if anyone could mollify Sylvie's pain, not when it had clearly penetrated every cell and molecule of her body. If someone took that pain away it would likely rip her in two. Or worse than that, make her disappear entirely.

\*\*\*

He avoided her for the next several days, even giving up his habit of watching her from his father's offices while she worked. It was puzzling to him that he could know something so intimate about a person, but feel farther carved out of her life than ever before. It made him grumpy and irritable. Feelings he was used to owning, but he had started to enjoy feeling uplifted and happy around Sylvie. He should have known better than to let himself get caught up in the drama of a girl.

"She would probably like flowers," Mabel said. The voice

startled Harold out of his self-loathing thoughts. Mabel was standing at the end of the kitchen table, her arms crossed against her chest in their usual fashion, her eyebrows raised as if exclaiming her point. "Most girls do."

He wanted to tell her he didn't know what she was talking about, but he lacked the energy to be evasive and argumentative. "Not her. She's different."

Mabel pulled out a chair and sat down, smoothing her dress underneath her thighs. The dress was made from a bolt of clearance periwinkle blue fabric. Harold thought the color clashed with her strawberry blond hair, but what did he know? He alternated between the same five shirts that he had worn since his last growth spurt in the tenth grade.

Mabel shook her head. "I don't think so. At least not as different as she would want you to think."

"She's so obstinate."

"Or lonely. It has to be hard for a girl not to have her mother. I don't know what I would do if anything happened to our mother."

"Everyone dies, Mabel. She can't use that as an excuse for being rude and belligerent."

"Well, then what's your excuse? You treat people that way all the time and from what I can tell you have quite a fine life. Maybe you should do her a favor and just leave her alone. Sounds to me like you ain't much of a catch. You're the one they throw back because you don't have potential."

Harold stayed at the kitchen table long after Mabel huffed away. He rubbed his thumb back and forth along the edge of the table, his own nervous habit, as he considered how he could reach Sylvie.

***

He approached her the next evening when he knew that she would be finishing up for the night and heading home to take care of her dad. She must have heard the rustle of his pants as he approached her because her back was turned to him when she said, "What is it,

Harold?"

"You don't have to be embarrassed."

She turned around to face him, head tilted to the side, a slightly bemused expression splashed across her face. "Why would I be embarrassed?"

"Because of what happened back at your, you know, back at your cabin."

Sylvie sighed and shook her head like a parent placating a child. "If anyone should be embarrassed it is you. You had no reason to be on my property."

"Yeah, but you were upset. It's not like you to be - " he searched for the word. "To be emotional."

"Why is it that men, or boys, think that one should be embarrassed to show emotion? Although I guess the better question is why should you get away with presuming that you know my nature?"

Harold resisted the urge to retort because he knew something nasty would tumble from his lips. Besides, he wanted to be kind. He had spent a great deal of time trying to devise a suitable plan for showing Sylvie how kind and caring he could be. Her sour attitude was ruining the attempt, but if he played along with her taunting it would only ruin it farther.

"I have a present for you," Harold said.

Sylvie regarded him warily. He wondered if they would ever move past this stage of mistrust and uncertainty. He was willing to take that step, but he wasn't sure she was as willing or even capable. "A present? It's not my birthday."

"You can get presents for occasions beside your birthday."

Sylvie brushed a stray hair out of her face and shrugged. "Honestly, I don't get presents for my birthday either. Last time I got a present was when my momma made me a dress just before she died. I hated dresses then and I hate them even more now. I sure hope the present you got me isn't a frilly dress. You would be better giving that to your sister."

Harold smiled. He liked it when Sylvie made jokes even if she didn't realize she was making them. He shook his head and assured her. "Sylvie, the last thing I would ever give you is a dress. Do you want to see your surprise?"

"I don't have a lot of time."

"It won't take long, at least not any longer than you want it to."

They walked back to his house, neither of them speaking. When he opened the front door, he motioned for her to follow him down the hall to the bathroom. He stopped just outside of the bathroom door, motioning inside. Sylvie raised her eyebrows. "I don't understand. You bought me a toilet?"

"No, look." He walked into the bathroom. Sylvie hung back, looking as confused as ever. He stepped over to the tub and glided his hand across the top, making waves. "It's a little cold, but if you turn these knobs," he gestured to the handles labeled "H" and "C", "you can add water and make it warmer."

"A bathtub?"

"I know it's not a claw foot tub, but it is still a warm bath. Mabel suggested I get you flowers, but I thought you would prefer something more practical."

Sylvie looked over her shoulder, down the hallway. "It's okay." Harold said. "My mom is playing bridge with the ladies from church and the old man is entertaining an out of town client at his office. I think they had dinner plans. Mabel might come home, but she won't bother you."

Sylvie shuffled her feet and gripped the doorframe. "I can't."

"Why not? Afraid you'll drown?" Harold chuckled.

Sylvie rolled her eyes. "Don't be clever. It doesn't suit you. Of course I'm not afraid of water."

"Then what?"

"It's too . . . too intimate, Harold. It wouldn't feel right, me being naked while you are in the house."

"You can shut the door."

"I know that, but it still feels wrong."

Harold stood up and handed her a towel. "I'll stay outside."

She didn't protest nor did she follow him outside. True to his word he waited for her on the porch. Time ticked by and he thought that maybe she had snuck past him, but then about an hour later he caught sight of a figure walking across the grass towards the woods. With sopping wet hair and equally wet clothing, Sylvie left without a word or a gesture of thanks.

***

Right after graduation in May, Harold received his truck. He couldn't believe that his father had purchased such a present for him. Mabel was astonished too and let her displeasure be heard.

"That is so excessive, father. Really?"

His father bent down to kiss Mabel's forehead and pat her head. "I would have bought one for you too but you refused to take your driver's test. I think you mentioned something about how you wouldn't need a license because your husband would do the driving?"

"I'll let you drive it," Harold said.

Mabel's eyes brightened. "Really?"

The corners of Harold's eyes crinkled as he laughed. "Hell, no!"

"Cretan," Mabel mumbled. "Well, if you think Sylvie will be impressed by that hunk of metal, think again. She doesn't care about material things like that."

It had been a few weeks since Harold presented her with his version of a present and he had noticed a shift in their relationship. She never acknowledged the bath incident and she still kept him at a distance, but the gap was closing little by little. She started to open up more to him and share bits of her life that he found incredible, such as the fact that she had never made a snow angel or written a letter to Santa. She didn't celebrate birthdays or holidays and she had never ridden in a car before.

"Never?" he questioned.

Sylvie slid off her tattered shoes and held up her feet. They were thick and rough on the bottoms with calluses that were years old and probably told just as many stories. "Look at my feet. They belong to the road, the grass, and the dirt. They have taken me many places, but never in a car."

Mabel was actually wrong about Sylvie's reaction to the red truck that he had decided to secretly name the Red Goblin. It was a foolish, childish nickname, but he couldn't help it. He felt like a super hero driving it.

"Wow," she exclaimed as she walked around the vehicle, seemingly examining every inch of the body and interior. She ran her hands along the wheel rail slowly; she let a single finger trail languorously around the steering wheel. "I never thought having a favorite color made sense, but I can see now that I love the color red. This is beautiful."

"Since when are cars beautiful?"

"There is beauty in so much of the world if you just take the time to look. We are all guilty of ignoring it."

Harold stared at her, mesmerized by how little she had experienced in life yet how much knowledge about the inner workings of the world she seemed to possess. She knew of life and death, sorrow and grief, yet at times she still seemed as innocent and fragile as a newborn.

"Do you want to take a ride?"

Her smile made him take a step back. It was so unlike her to show such an exuberance of emotion that his first instinct was that she was snarling at him. It took him a second to realize this was an expression of excitement. "Yes!"

"Um, okay. Well, hop in."

They lumbered down Main Street barely reaching a speed of fifteen miles per hour. Sylvie messed with the radio like a child, turning the knob, alternating between static and music. She stuck her feet out the window, slouching down into the seat. "The wind feels nice. Can it go faster?"

They sped down the back roads over Payne Bridge. Harold pushed hard on the accelerator urging the truck to go faster and faster. Sylvie giggled each time the truck reached a higher speed and the wind knotted her hair around her face. Sylvie's jubilance encouraged Harold's recklessness. When they had driven about four miles out of town, Harold stopped the car in the middle of the dirt road.

"Did we run out of gas?" Sylvie asked. Her hair was plastered to one side of her face. She had traces of dirt on her forehead, mixed with sweat. Harold couldn't hold back his feelings any longer. He leaned across the seat, cupped the back of her head in his hand with his fingers entwined in her hair, and kissed her. It wasn't the most romantic kiss in the world, certainly not worthy of the silver screen but it made Harold feel light and elated. He didn't notice that Sylvie hadn't kissed him back.

When he pulled away she was staring at him, her fingers touching her lips. "Why did you do that?"

"I wanted to for a long time."

"You shouldn't have."

"Why?"

She didn't answer him. Instead she hopped out of the truck and started walking back towards town. Harold jumped out of the cab and yelled after her. "Where are you going?"

"Back."

"Back where?" Harold asked when he had caught up to her. She kept walking. He grabbed her shoulder, forcing her to stop.

"Back to when you didn't do that."

"I'm sorry. I take it back."

"It's not possible to take it back."

"Well, I won't do it again."

"Yes, you will." She looked at him, daring him.

Some guys Harold knew were smooth with the girls. They knew how to take command of a situation, but he wasn't like that. At least he never thought he was like that, until now. Until now, when he felt fury and passion ignite and turn him into the creature he loathed most. He wasn't gentle this time. He grabbed Sylvie by the shoulders and kissed her hard. His teeth grinded against her teeth as his kisses became more urgent. He pulled away and looked in her eyes. "Don't walk home."

She got back into the cab with him and he kissed her again. He slipped the fingers of his right hand under the collar of her shirt, while his left hand rested on her hipbone. "Do you love me?" he asked as he proceeded to climb on top of her. He waited for her to tell him to stop. She didn't. He secretly wished she would because he had no clue what he was doing.

Instead she took Harold's face in her hands and forced him to look into her eyes as he panted above her. "No, Harold. I don't love you."

***

If Harold had been confused about their relationship prior to the day on the country road, his confusion didn't cease as the days progressed. He and Sylvie continued their relationship, which was based on his admiration and her amusement. It pained him that Sylvie had told him she didn't love him, but he didn't exactly care. She continued to be with him in every sense of the word. He was sure that her feelings would change when he told her he was leaving in a few short weeks to join the Browns on the road. It created a sense of excitement in him to think that finally he might get an emotional response from Sylvie.

"I think that's great," she said as they lay in the back of his truck on a soft bed of hay.

"You think it's great that I'm going away?"

"Yes, it's a great opportunity and you have always wanted to play ball. Why would I want you to stay here?"

Harold propped himself up on his elbow and studied her. Was she joking? "Because of you and I."

Sylvie sighed that exasperated parental sigh. "Harold, don't make this more than it is."

"I thought this was something special we had."

Sylvie sat up and brushed the hay off of her skirt. "No, it isn't. This is just killing time."

"That is the meanest thing I have ever heard anyone say. Why are you so heartless?"

"I'm not heartless. I'm honest. I told you I didn't love you. I don't love you; therefore, I have no reason to believe that you are mine to regret or to miss."

Harold took his frustration and anger out on the road ahead of him. For the past several weeks since Sylvie had uttered that heartless confession, he had avoided her, opting instead to ravage the countryside, running his truck as fast as it would take him. He wasn't sure where he thought he would get with these antics, but he didn't care; pushing hard on the accelerator, feeling the road bounce beneath him, and listening to the gravel crunch in his wake kept him sane. Or at least a foot away from insanity.

He had nothing but time to kill now, a stupid thought considering what Sylvie had said to him the last time he had seen her. He couldn't believe that she could be that callous and cold-hearted. Wasn't that the way the man was supposed to act? She had basically taken his dick, twisted it into a pathetic heart, and then left him begging her to love him. That was a pathetic spot to be as a man, he convinced himself. If that was the way she wanted to be then he was done with Sylvie Day.

His father had warned him to ease up on the pedal. Harold had assured him he would, but had no intention of keeping that promise. He figured if he could take this truck as far and as fast as he could for the next couple weeks before he met up with Baker and the team then he wouldn't lose his grip. He wouldn't find himself in the wee hours of the morning, standing in front of Sylvie's door, asking her to reconsider her feelings. But it's a nonsensical thing to think that one can trade one reckless behavior for another and get away with it.

Nearly three weeks to the day that Sylvie trampled over his

feelings, Harold lost control. Not on purpose, but it didn't really matter because the results were equally as damaging no matter how you looked at it. He had found a bottle of the elder Klein's Wild Turkey bourbon, a bottle that was stored under the kitchen and saved for special guests and those long days when nothing would heal the elder's dismay at the system quite as well as a shot of whiskey. Harold, Jr. grabbed the bottle and tucked it into the back of his jeans, but not before Mabel caught him. She started to open her mouth to purge a rude comment, but he gave her a look that stopped her in her tracks. Instead she shook her head and walked away. Maybe things would have turned out differently if Harold hadn't given her the death stare. Maybe, but fate has a way of lining things up just right. At least that is how he would justify his actions in the years that followed.

With the Wild Turkey pressing into his hipbone he climbed into the cab of his truck. He withdrew the bottle, sniffed the contents, and took a huge swallow before he lost his nerve. The heat tore at his throat, but warmed his insides. Instantly, he felt brave. He stared at the gold liquid in the bottle and took another swig, this time a longer drink, letting the alcohol numb the fire. He placed the bottle in the seat beside him and started the engine. He knew exactly what he was going to do. He was going to drive to Sylvie's and make her see things from his point of view. He was going to make her love him. He had convinced himself it was the right thing to do. She had given him every bit of her. She belonged to him. They belonged together.

His truck was bouncing along the open, gravel roads that led out of town. At the last minute he decided to take a detour. He needed a few extra minutes to gather his liquid courage as well as his thoughts. He noticed it was getting harder to steer the truck, keep it steady. He couldn't imagine why the wheel refused to stay centered, but then again he had never drank Wild Turkey while driving so what did he know? He shook his head a few times trying to clear his mind and focus.

The truck came upon the railroad tracks that divided the townies from the countries. Once he crossed the tracks he could circle around and approach Sylvie's cabin from the opposite side. It was nearly twilight, which meant she would be home, presumably fixing dinner or more than likely casting spells because only a witch could possibly conjure up enough meanness to tear a young man's heart in two like she did. Harold was aware that the thoughts forming in his head were incoherent and misguided, but he wasn't sober enough to care.

As the Dodge truck skipped over the tracks, Harold heard a pop and the car lurched forward. *What the hell*, he thought. He climbed out of the cab and saw his front driver's side tire completely flattened.

"Shit," he yelled at the top of lungs. He looked around for help. The drunken railroad crowd must have been getting high off of moonshine somewhere else. Well, what was he supposed to do? He had to get this truck off the tracks. He didn't know the train schedule, but you could hear the train whistles at all hours of the day so he knew that his truck wouldn't be safe here for long.

"You's need some help, son?" a man's voice asked. Harold squinted towards the sound of the voice, certain he was hallucinating because he had been alone two seconds earlier. "You don't want to leave that here," the voice insisted.

"Who's there?" Harold asked. His words came out garbled, unintelligible.

"Name's Gold. You Klein's boy?"

Harold watched Sylvie's dad emerge from the shadows as the sun continued to disappear. He was shorter than Harold and shuffled rather than walked. His face was weathered and wrinkled from spending hours in the sun, walking aimlessly around town, searching for something to keep him busy. When he spoke Harold noticed the gaps where teeth used to reside. For a second Harold felt sorry for him, but then just as quickly pushed the feelings aside because he was the father of the girl who had broken his heart. He owed him nothing; no feelings whatsoever.

"Get out of here, old man. I ain't need your help."

"I hate to argue with you son, but I think you do. You see, that there seven o'clock train is never late. If you have a watch, I think you will see that you don't have much time to save that pretty vehicle." Harold wished at that moment that his father had given him a watch, then he wouldn't be in this mess. "Get in there and put her in neutral. We'll give her a little push."

Harold stood there contemplating letting Gold help him. He didn't need his help. Or did he?

"Why's you standing there like that boy? You been in the sauce? I think you have. I know how that feels, but shake it off. We got to get that truck off these here tracks. "

Reluctantly, Harold climbed back into the cab. He put the car in neutral and then hopped back down. "Now what?"

Gold grinned, revealing even more missing teeth. "Well, we push. Come on. Let's get this off the track."

Together they began to push, but a scrap of a man and a drunken teenage boy were no match for a hunk of steel. It took them several attempts and just when they had managed to move the truck a fraction of an inch across the track two things happened that shifted the Earth on its axis, revealing a new reality that would change the course of Harold's life forever. The tracks started to vibrate under Harold's feet. A distant rumble could be heard. "The train," Harold stated.

Gold nodded and started to move back and concede defeat. "Looks like she's a goner, boy. Best let the steel bullet take her away."

Harold stared at him. "What? Are you mad? No, help me. You promised to help me."

"I offered help, but didn't make promises. Sometimes you just got to let things go."

Harold shook his head fiercely back and forth again, convinced he was making things up. Was Gold talking about the truck or Sylvie? "Help me!" Harold screamed as the rumble grew louder.

The older man shook his head and threw up his hands. "Steel bullet has no choice but to take her away. We better move off the track." Gold went to move, but pitched forward instead. He tried to stand and move in Harold's direction, but couldn't release his foot. It was stuck under the railroad ties. The train was close enough now to see its single headlight, growing larger and larger.

"Take your foot out of your shoe," Harold yelled over the roar of the approaching train.

"I am not losing this shoe. These the only pair I own. What will Sylvie say?"

Harold glanced from the shoe to the train coming closer and closer. "Are you out of your mind? Take the goddamn shoe off."

Harold frantically started pulling the older man by his shoulders trying to force his foot out of the shoe, but for such a delicate man he put up a struggle. By now the tracks were shaking wildly. As Harold continued to struggle to release the man from his shoe, Gold leaned back, his stale breath permeating the air between them and spoke clearly, "Maybe it will just take the foot, but if it takes me tell Sylvie she's got her momma's eyes."

What happened next Harold would never be able to fully reconcile. He remembered the rush of air as the train hurdled past. He heard the crunching of metal on metal and suddenly felt lighter. He was flying. Yes, he was flying faster than the steel bullet could race down the track. At that moment he felt peaceful. Then he felt nothing because the world became black.

Harold would awaken four days later in a city hospital, surrounded by his wearied father, sniveling mother, and wide-eyed sister. He would find himself in a hospital bed with a fractured hip that had been inundated with bone shrapnel when his car, or parts of it at least, had been thrown on top of him. He would spend two weeks in the hospital laying in that bed, waiting to be released, wondering where Sylvie was and wondering if she blamed him for her father's death. Here's what Harold would not know, at least not for many, many years.

As he lay in that hospital bed, being pumped full of morphine, slowly accepting that his dreams and ambitions of being a ball player were gone, he would not know that Sylvie had buried what was left her father in the same place as her mother and stillborn brother without fanfare or help. He would not realize that Sylvie had discovered she was pregnant two days after they argued as they lay in the bed of hay in the back of his truck. He would not know that she knew he had led everyone to believe that her father had been killed because he had been drunk that night and not the other way around. What Harold didn't know, but what Sylvie had known, is that her father wouldn't have been sipping Wild Turkey or anything for that matter. People assumed her daddy had been nothing but a blithering drunk for all her life and while some of that was true, he hadn't touched a drop of whiskey in the three months since he had been diagnosed with intestinal cancer. The truth is her daddy would have been dead in several months anyway, but Harold didn't know this.

What Harold had no way of knowing was that Sylvie would never come visit him in that hospital. She would pack a single bag and leave Marion for the next thirteen years. She would lead a completely different life in the big city. She would give up their daughter to a family that would raise her by two parents who loved her and each other immensely.

Whatever Harold thought he knew, the truth was that Sylvie would never love him. What Harold wouldn't understand is that a baby deserved better. Lastly, what Harold didn't know, and Sylvie for that matter, was that for the next several years they would live just three blocks apart in that big city, never once running into each other, but that in the years to come they would find themselves a part of each other's lives once more, facing the same struggles of life and death and truth.

# Part Two

*"August rain: the best of the summer gone, and the new fall not yet born. The odd uneven time."*

-Sylvia Plath

## Chapter 5 – Addie Cullins
### *1978*

Addie Cullins parked across the street from Sylvie's medical office, watching women in all stages of pregnancy and life meander in and out of the doors. She glanced at the cheap watch on her right hand as she took a long drag off the cigarette dangling between her left fingers. She had been sitting in the 1970 Mercury Marquis for nearly two hours and sweat had begun to trickle into the small of her back. She smelled bad and she only had two cigarettes left. It appeared that the whole blessed town of Marion had decided to make appointments today; the day that she and Sylvie needed to have a serious talk with each other.

A simple phone call, an easy request to make an appointment, is all she would have needed to do to avoid this conundrum of waiting and decomposing prematurely in her vehicle, but that would have alerted Bart. Alerting Bart is not what Addie intended to do, now or ever. The nicotine worked its way through her nervous system, but it failed to calm her; she still tapped her chipped fingernail on the steering wheel over and over again. Her foot mimicked the rhythm. She was running out of time. Bart's shift would be over in less than an hour and he would be expecting her to show up at Millie's, the low-rent dive bar that she heard had been a more respectable place a few decades ago.

Addie finished off the cigarette, flicked it out the window, and smoothed her hair. She didn't quite know why she had to put on airs for Sylvie – excuse her, Dr. Day, – but she knew that to get what she needed she would have to be presentable. Her history with Sylvie, not to mention her current reputation, demanded that she make a good case for herself.

Crossing the street, Addie looked down at her feet to avoid Margaret Lin who had just exited the building. The woman looked like she was about to pop that baby out any minute. Although Addie avoided her now, she still saw her in town often, smiling and carrying on about how excited she was to give her Jia a new sibling. At four years old, Jia was the same age as Addie's youngest, Bobby, and Sylvie's girl, Charlotte. Addie contemplated what it would be like to walk with your head held high and excited about the birth of a new child. Each time she had been pregnant she only felt shame and embarrassment. The last thing she wanted was to be a mother again.

Instead of going in the front she went around the back of the brick building, gingerly stepping around rocks, a few broken beer bottles, and a stray flyer for an upcoming fair that had managed to escape someone's hand. Addie knocked two times on the backdoor. She counted to ten and knocked two more times, harder and urgently. The door opened hesitantly. Sylvie emerged looking concerned at first, then suspicious as she looked around Addie to see if she was alone. Once she was satisfied that Addie was the only threat, she relaxed against the doorframe and crossed her arms against her chest.

"I have a front door, Addie. This is the door we use to take out the trash."

"This isn't a front door type of discussion," Addie said. The sweat that had lingered at the base of her spine while she was in the car had started to trickle between her buttocks and drip down her legs.

"Would you like to come in?" Sylvie asked.

Addie nodded. Sylvie stepped aside to let her pass then motioned for her to sit down in a chair shoved into the corner.

Medical supplies were stacked on shelves and the faint smell of antiseptic lingered in the air. She smoothed her skirt under her thighs, doing the best she could to appear calm. Her hands had begun to shake. She wished she had taken a drag or two off a cigarette before knocking on the door.

"Do you consult with all your patients in the medical supply closet?" she asked, attempting a smile, trying to appear cordial and non-threatening.

"You haven't been a patient of mine for quite some time, Addie. And since this is not a front door conversation it probably doesn't require an examination room."

Addie was quiet for several seconds, maybe even minutes. Sylvie didn't rush her, which Addie appreciated, but she still felt squeamish as Sylvie continued to stare at her. Finally, she broke her silence. "I need some help."

"Most people do."

"It's Bart. No, it's me. See, he hasn't been interested in me for a long time. At least not in the husbandly way, but lately all he wants to do is . . . Well, you know."

Sylvie narrowed her eyes. "Go on."

"He keeps me on a tight budget: liquor, food, and stuff for the kids; in that order, too. No exceptions. It means I can't pay for things that I need to make sure I am never your patient again, Sylvie."

"It's Dr. Day."

Addie cocked her head in a questioning manner. "Yes, I just thought since –"

"You thought wrong," Sylvie interrupted.

"Okay. So can you help?"

"With what?"

Addie swallowed hard. She had known Sylvie for several years. They had even been on friendly terms for a while; she, Mabel, and Sylvie. But that seemed ages ago. Now she had no friends, mostly thanks to Bart's reputation and poor choices. Nonetheless, Sylvie's tone and insistence that she spell it out for her made her angry. Who did this woman think she was? Did she think she was better than her? Not too long ago, Sylvie lived on the wrong side of public opinion too. But, Addie figured, a fancy degree and a reinvented life could right all those wrong tracks.

"I can't get pregnant again. I need something."

"Birth control?"

"If that's what you call it."

"I take it that husband of yours wouldn't be too pleased to find you are limiting his ability to repopulate the world with Cullins blood?"

Addie snorted. "He don't care about none of the kids that we make or I pop out. What he cares about is controlling the damn lot of us. I am going to be 43 in a few months. I thought that I wouldn't have to worry about having any more kids. Aren't I supposed to be worrying about the change and being a Grandma? Hell, Elvira is going to be 22 next month."

"All women's bodies are different," Sylvie lectured. "It could be years before your body makes that transition."

"Exactly. So, what I need now is to make sure all this baby making stuff stops. And since I can't get Bart to ease up on his urges, I need to take measures into my own hands. Surely I am not the first desperate woman to come to you asking for a little help?"

Sylvie regarded her for a moment then walked over to one of the shelves. She returned with two packets of pills. "I can get you started. It will take about a month before you can have intercourse without worrying about getting pregnant. So you'll have to be careful until then. But I can't help you beyond this. There's a Planned Parenthood in St. Louis. You should be able to get what you need from them, but you'll have to be able to pay something and you will need to have an exam."

"Thank you, Sylvie. You are saving my life."

"I hardly believe that, especially with that man in your life. You'd be best to pack up those kids and get the hell out of here."

Addie looked at Sylvie in disbelief. Here was the pompous

attitude she had been expecting. "And go where? It's not that easy, Sylvie. Some of us don't have the education or the means to find a job that will put food on the table and a roof over our heads if we ain't attached to our men."

Sylvie nodded. "I am under no illusions that life is sugar-coated. We all do what we have to do. But this is all I can do for you. I can't help you beyond this. You understand?"

Addie stood, putting the small silver packets in her purse. The packet of cigarettes fell out on the floor. Sylvie reached down and picked them up. She turned to walk away from Addie, tossing the cigarettes in the trashcan and without turning back around said, "You take care of yourself, Addie."

## Chapter 6 – Charlotte
*Present Day*

"He's lying," I said as Nick and I drove back to the farmhouse. My doubt and disbelief was almost palpable, hanging heavy and dangerous like invisible gas from a chemical weapon – and just as deadly.

"Maybe not," Nick suggested.

"Of course he's lying," I insisted.

"Okay. Fine, he's lying."

"What? You think he's telling the truth?"

"Why wouldn't he?" Nick suggested.

I rolled my eyes, throwing my head back against the seat. "It doesn't make sense. I can't even imagine her with any other man than my dad. She loved him so much. Only him . . . that's why she never remarried."

"This was a long time before that, Charlotte; at least according to Harold."

"I know. I'm just trying to rationalize it. She just never seemed fond of that man – ever. And the way he described her as cold and callous, well that doesn't sound like the woman I knew as my mother. That certainly isn't a woman who had an entire community show up on her lawn to say goodbye. Does it?"

Nick shrugged. "I don't know, Charlotte. Maybe she was a different woman before she had you. People are complicated and no one is perfect."

I looked out the window, refusing to acknowledge Nick's ridiculous assumption that I thought the world was rose-colored and good people's shit smelled like lilies. Of course I knew that people had many sides. I certainly was a much different person than before I met Nick. I pushed those thoughts out of my head as quickly as they entered. I didn't want to think about that now. I couldn't. I had to focus.

"I just can't believe she never told me."

"Let me ask you a question. Are you upset that she didn't tell you or that you weren't her only child?"

"Maybe a little of both."

"So, what now? Do we look for her?"

"Should we?"

Nick glanced at with his eyebrows raised, a visual question mark. "Aren't you the least bit curious?"

"Why should I be?"

Nick sighed. "Really? Come on, Charlotte. You aren't the least bit interested in learning more about this woman who shares half your blood?"

I shifted in my seat to face him while he drove. "And Harold's blood, too. Don't forget that. She's half him. What if she is mean-spirited, awkward, and rude?"

"Then she is, but I just thought you might like the idea of knowing that you have family out there. You're not alone," he said.

"I'm not alone," I reminded him. "I have you and this baby."

"Yeah, but think of this. You could have nieces or nephews, too."

"Yes, but they would probably be our age. How weird would that be? I mean, Nick, this woman who is my sister is old enough to be my mother. That's strange."

Nick pulled off the road into the Quik Stop. The fuel sensor had begun to ping, a sound that drove my usually mellow husband completely insane. He pulled up to the pump, turned the ignition off, and looked over at me. "You know what I think? I think you are purposely making this into a strange situation. Why not give it a chance? Your mom may not have been completely honest with you while she was alive, but she didn't want to die without you having this knowledge at some point. Just think about it."

When he got out of the car, I closed my eyes and cursed his reasoning. He was right after all.

***

That same summer I asked Mom about voodoo was also the summer I spent planting seeds throughout the yard wherever my heart desired. My mom hadn't noticed or she figured I was just playing around. That is until green bean plants and tomato plants started popping up in curious places.

"I'm trying to grow a baby." I told her when she asked why there were odd vegetables sprouting in the front yard.

"A baby? Why on Earth do you want a baby?" Mom had asked.

"Because they smell good and they make funny faces." I had been spending time with Jia after school while Mom finished up her appointments for the day. We would spend hours letting Jia's little brother entertain us with goofy smiles and silly baby sounds.

"Well, Charlotte. I don't know about that. How's the planting going? Have any babies shown up?"

I shook my head sadly. "No, not yet, but maybe tomorrow. When the baby does show up I want to name him Ollie."

"Sounds like you have it all figured out. Where will Ollie sleep?"

I remember giving my mother an incredulous look and then simply stating, "In the garden of course. Where else would he sleep?"

I remember that Mom had laughed real hard and I laughed along to please her, but I wasn't quite sure what I had said that was so funny.

About three weeks later, late one night when I had already been asleep for hours, Mom and I were awoken by a knock on the front door. I started to come down the stairs, but she told me to stay put. "Go to your room, Charlotte," she whispered.

Of course, I didn't listen. I snuck down the steps and saw my mom reaching high up in the coat closet, pulling out a shotgun. I caught my breath. I had never seen a gun before and I certainly didn't know that my mom owned one. With the gun at her side, she walked to the door. "Who is it?" she hollered.

"Please, please ma'am. Please let me in. I am with child," the voice said.

Mom peeked out the window and then quickly put the gun down. She yanked open the door and ushered a tall, emaciated woman the color of coffee into our home. My eyes grew large at the sight of this strange creature. Living in a rural community didn't expose me to many people who were different than I was. This was the first black person I had ever seen.

With one hand she reached out to grab my mother's shoulder, while her other hand grasped the bottom of her swollen stomach. When she entered the house she was nearly a foot taller than my mother, but as pain overtook her body she hunched over and was face to face with her. Without hesitation or concern about what people may say, my mother led the woman to the fireplace. She removed the cushions from the couch and arranged them on the floor like a mattress. She helped the woman lie back on the cushions and then reached between her legs.

"Oh, my," I heard her say. "You got here just in time. This isn't going to take long at all. Here's what I need you to do. Hold your breath and then on the count of three I want you to blow out that breath and push as hard as you can. You understand?" The woman nodded frantically. "Okay, here we go. One . . . two . . . three!"

The woman let out more than air. She elicited a primal

scream that sounded like an animal was dying. I covered my ears, scared that she would die because I couldn't imagine someone in so much pain doing anything else but dying. My mom wiped her forehead with the back of her hand and said, "Almost there. One more time, okay? One . . . two . . . three!"

"The grace of youth," my mother whispered as the baby emerged from between this strange, dark woman's legs. This woman who, only minutes earlier, had wandered into our home, starved and cold and very much ready to deliver her child. I stood shivering on the stairs, gripping the stair rail afraid to blink, move, or breathe, unsure if I was witnessing a miracle or observing something grotesque and inhuman. But now, as I watched a baby slide into my mother's arms with a natural suppleness that only a newborn could possess, I decided that this was indeed a miracle. I may have been only five years old, but even I knew that the grace of God had laid his hand upon the four of us in that room.

My mom looked up at me, her eyes bright and alive, and urgently called to me. "Charlotte, come. It's okay."

I slowly released my grip on the stair rail and shuffled my feet along the hardwood floor. As I came to stand next to my mother, I watched as the baby girl, only seconds old, stretched her arms high over her head and exhaled a long breath that flowed from her tiny, puckered lips as easy and naturally as if breathing were a right, not a given. What happened next I can't recall, but I do remember never doubting the strength that a body can possess and the miracles it could produce. I also realized at that moment that babies didn't come from plants.

## Chapter 7 – Addie
### *1978*

Finding solace in her daily life was never easy. If she wasn't dealing with a brood of offspring fighting for her every last minute of attention, she was fighting off her husband; a man who could be seductive and gentle one minute, but cruel and unrelenting the next. The one place in this suffocating town that Addie was able to find a nugget of peace was at St. Roberts Catholic Church.

Addie had been raised a southern Baptist by her God-fearing parents, Bert and Nellie Cross, but decided to find Jesus in a different way when she met Bart at a Baptist revival just south of Memphis. She should have known nothing good would come from meeting a man who claimed to be a devout Catholic, yet convinced her that the best way to get closer to God wasn't chanting and praying under a tent. The best way, he said, was to share a pint of whiskey and a twin-sized mattress at The Flamingo Inn. At the age of 19, Addie didn't have a clue what it meant to walk with shame. But several pints of whiskey and enough tussles later to produce five children, Addie knew quite a bit about what it meant to live *with* shame on a daily basis.

Of all the things that Bart had convinced her to do over the years, insisting that she convert to his religion was actually a blessing in disguise. Although her parents were completely dismayed that their daughter would be drafted into a religion that they deemed unworthy of a true Christian, Addie felt right at home. She liked the rituals and melodic nature of the hymns. Attending church on Sunday at St. Roberts was serene, unlike the revivals and services she attended as a child, which were energetic, but set her nerves on fire. With all the other variables in her life that could wear on her nerves, Addie craved the calmness of St. Roberts.

This need for peacefulness led her to volunteer to clean the church on Tuesday evenings between seven and nine. It was the only thing that Bart let her do that wasn't closely monitored or criticized. She looked forward to Tuesday more than anything else in the world. The church doors were never locked and anyone was welcome walk through the front doors, but no one ever stepped foot in the church on those evenings. For two hours, Addie hummed hymns while she wiped down the pews with soap and water. She polished the stained glass windows as far as she could reach while she prayed the Hail Mary. Each time she crossed the altar to replenish her cleaning supplies she would make the sign of the cross and genuflect. But, the first Tuesday she went back to clean the church after meeting with Sylvie, things weren't the same.

Instead of humming the hymns and saying her prayers, she sat in the front pew turning the small silver packets over and over in her hands. One pill was missing and she already felt like a sinner. Addie didn't completely cross entirely over into the Catholic faith. One thing she refused to do was go to confession and ask for penance. There were plenty of bad things that she had done over the past twenty or more years and most of them were because of her relationship with Bart, but she never understood what telling a priest could do to absolve her of the pain attached to those choices. She also didn't believe that all of her choices were wrong.

If Bart discovered that Addie had visited Sylvie for the little white pills, well, she shuddered to think about how unhinged he may become. He had certainly unleashed his fury on her before for little things: ripping a handful of hair from her scalp when she burned the chicken two weeks after they were married; leaving a trail of bruises up and down her spine when she was ten minutes late picking him up. She could go on and on. All anyone had to do was take one look at her naked body to see why she might be scared of her husband. It was one of the many reasons that Addie couldn't be Sylvie's patient.

But these little white pills were a completely different danger. Two things would occur if Bart were to discover that she had them. The first would be the accusations that she was screwing around on him. In all honestly, Addie already knew the punishment that always accompanied this accusation; a backhand to the face, quick and to the point. She could handle that. The second is the one she feared the most. Bart was twisted and he applied his twisted way of thinking to everything in life, including his insistence that they produce the children God meant for them to produce. That meant no birth control.

Five years earlier, during a rare three-month period in which Bart had been uncharacteristically gracious, Addie had pleaded with her husband to let her take birth control. The house was unusually quiet because Addie's parents had rolled into town on their way to an event in Iowa later in the week and they had offered to take the kids into town for ice cream. There was a new ice cream parlor that had opened up and the kids had been eager to go for months, even when the weather got too cold for ice cream to taste good. But money was always sparse. When Addie's parents offered to foot the bill, the kids ran out to their grandparent's station wagon and Bart said not a word, just sat down to eat his dinner that had grown cold.

"If I pop one more kid out of this body, we ain't gonna be able to eat, " she said.

"Are you telling me I can't support my family?" Bart replied. His voice was steady and with his unusually docile behavior over the past few months, she felt encouraged to continue.

"Of course that's not what I am saying. It's just that four children is plenty and neither one of us is getting any younger."

"We have the children that God intends for us to have."

"That's rubbish," Addie said.

Bart put down his fork and looked her in the eye. For a second she had almost dropped the subject, but that stubborn streak that had played a part in her rebellion all those years ago that led to this life with Bart boiled under her skin. "That's rubbish," she said again.

"You better watch your mouth, Addie. I don't think I like where this is headed. You're gonna get me angry."

"We don't need any more kids."

Bart stood up. "You sayin' we don't need any more of my offspring?"

"What? No. That's not what I'm saying. You're talking crazy. I just don't want to be pregnant anymore. I want to enjoy life and not worry about babies and diapers. Four kids is enough. I have a right- "

"You have no rights, but you do have obligations and duties; to me and to the Lord."

"Really? What are your obligations? Are you obliged to treat your wife with respect? Are you expected to come home every night sober and ready to be a father? Instead, you're putting your cock in every whore from here to St. Louis. You don't have to worry about a lack of offspring. I am pretty certain you leave a trail of sad, fatherless kids wherever you go."

Addie had known she crossed a line. Her heart raced as she watched Bart roll and unroll his tongue the way he did when he was getting ready to dole out punishment. She shuffled back away from him, bracing herself against the kitchen sink, preparing herself for his fury. Addie was used to the physical abuse: punching, hitting, kicking, biting. Biting was the worse. It was so primal and incredibly intimate that it scared her more than any other type of physical violence Bart chose. But what came next she had not been prepared for.

Bart approached her slowly. He kept his eyes on her like prey that he couldn't afford to lose sight of. He stood in front of her, bending his head so his nose was directly in front of hers. She felt his hot breath on her face. He reached up, gingerly touching her hair, tracing his finger along her jawline. His forefinger traveled back up along her ear. She had pulled her hair back into a low ponytail that morning and he reached back to undo it. The way that he touched her in that moment made her feel, against all logic and everything she knew about her husband, hopeful that life maybe could be calm and peaceful, that maybe her words had reached some logical, kind part of Bart's soul. In the moments that passed before what happened next, she thought that maybe she and Bart could be happy together; that the last 19 years together could be erased and they could fall in love.

But then Bart slammed his forehead into her so hard that she swore she felt her brain shake against her skull.

Dazed, she fell to the floor, fighting the urge to vomit. Unfortunately, Bart's assault wasn't over. He grabbed her by the hair, dragging her from the kitchen into their bedroom. His large hands encircled her neck and he tossed her like a rag doll onto the bed. What came next, Addie didn't like to remember. There were many things Bart did that a husband shouldn't do to his wife, but what happened in that room was something she never imagined was possible. But in the end it didn't matter what she wanted or what she thought, because nine months later Bobby was born.

So as Addie sat in the front pew she prayed to Jesus and to Mary and all the saints she could think of to help her decide what to do. But all she could hear was Bart's angry voice the night he raped her and she conceived their child, screaming at her over and over that she would never defy him again. With those words in her head, she finished cleaning the church and on her way out the door she threw away the silver packets.

## Chapter 8 – Charlotte
*Present Day*

Did it surprise me that my mom had secrets? I would be lying if I said it did. Everyone has secrets. That is human nature. The secrets that we keep usually develop out of fear; fear of being less than worthy in another person's eyes. When I chose to look at the current situation in this way the pain of being lied to for the past 36 years weakened a bit, but it still throbbed beneath my skin, threating to explode.

Nick had left me at the farmhouse while he went back into town to grab some groceries. I was happy for the space, but was feeling anxious alone in this house again. For so many years, I had loved and loathed the quaintness of our home. As a child I found the wide-open spaces and the vast amount of acreage to be just the right amount of space for my wild and adventurous personality. When Granny and Grandpa Day were still alive they would bring their Golden Retriever, Lucky, to visit and he and I would run in circles for hours and hours. But then Lucky got too old to run, Granny and Grandpa succumbed to old age and the various forms of cancer that come with it, and I grew into a teenager who found those wide open spaces constricting.

We don't just lie to other people. We lie to ourselves, too. The first time I lied to myself was when I was 17 years old and was convinced that I had fallen in love with Bobby Cullins. Never mind that I knew he was a loathsome person; the kind of person that doted on you one minute, but didn't treat you with an ounce of consideration the next. He wasn't what you would call loveable and, although nearly all the girls in my high school were madly in love with him, he wasn't all that attractive either. He was a lanky teenage boy with a smattering of pimples across his forehead, shaggy hair that always seemed in need of a washing, and a generally bad attitude. But he was part of my youthful rebellion.

The first time that I walked through the front door of the farmhouse with Bobby, his hands in the back pocket of my jeans, was the first time I saw my mother truly rattled. She had been putting away the dishes that I had forgotten to wash that morning before I went to school, one of my few chores but the one I hated the most. She looked at him first, then back to me and pulled herself upright, making herself as tall as was humanely possible for such a slight woman.

"Charlotte?" she questioned. Her tone was a blend of anger and confusion. It wasn't surprising that she had reservations about Bobby and it wasn't a secret that she believed his family – or what was left of it – was still nothing but trouble.

Looking back, I think I always knew that I was really only with Bobby because I knew it would get my mother riled up. But still I balked when she tried to protect me from this relationship she knew was no good for me. I was dumb and naïve, too wrapped up in my own childish ways to understand that parents usually have a reason for putting up force fields around their children to protect them from bad influences. Unfortunately for my mother and later for me, the force field was penetrable.

"Can Bobby hang out here for a while? We were going to listen to some old mixed tapes up in my room."

"And in a minute I am going to outside to milk a cow for fresh milk."

I rolled my eyes at my mom's ridiculous attempt at a joke. It was far from amusing. However, Bobby didn't get it. He scratched his head, creating a halo of dandruff that floated around him. "You ain't got no cow, Mrs. D."

Mom had taken a deep breath, no doubt counting to ten before she replied. "We do not have a cow, young man. How wise of you to take notice. It is my way of informing you and my daughter that if you would like to listen to your mixed tapes you can do so in the living room or grab a handful of batteries and go on the porch. Boys are not allowed in Charlotte's room."

"Whatever," Bobby said.

"Yes, ma'am," Mom had said.

"What?" Bobby asked.

"Yes, ma'm. That is how you address me when you are speaking to me. Do you understand?"

Bobby had stayed for an hour then left without incident. As soon as Bobby left, I stormed into the house, livid and on fire. Mom was sitting in my dad's ratty old armchair next to fireplace reading a Nancy Drew mystery. I never understood why she enjoyed those books so much, but she told me that my dad had introduced her to them when they first started dating. *The Clue of the Broken Locket*, the book she had open in her lap, was a birthday present from him their first Christmas together.

"How was your visit?" she asked without looking up.

"Why can't you just be like other mothers?" I had asked.

At first she didn't respond and I thought she would ignore me. But instead, she took off her glasses, shut her book, and peered up at me. Her face was calm, always grace under pressure. Mine was enflamed as my temper began to soar. "How does that work?"

"Work? It works really easily when you treat people with kindness. You have always preached kindness to me, but you were quite rude to Bobby."

"Kindness is a two way street, my dear. That young man has a lot to learn about giving and receiving kindness. Do you think you are going to change him?"

"Why would I want to change him? He's perfect just the way he is."

"He comes from a long line of bad apples, Charlotte. I am only trying to protect you. With so many other eligible young men in town, why take your chances on one that already has so much going against him?"

"The only person against him is you."

"I'm not against him, Charlotte. I am simply looking out for you."

"Why can't you just be normal?"

"What's normal dear? Acting the same as everyone else just for the hell of it?"

"Don't you know that people talk?" I asked.

"You mean gossip?"

"Call it whatever you want, but people talk about you. About us."

My mom cocked her head to the side as if this were news to her, which it probably was because she rarely gave much thought or notice to anything outside of this house or her practice. "What do they say?"

I hadn't been expecting her to challenge me, so I wasn't prepared for her to call my bluff. "They say you never remarried because you have a secret lover," I lied.

Mom laughed boisterously. "Really? Because I have time for secret trysts at the inn? That's fine, Charlotte. Let people think what they want. It doesn't affect us."

"They say you're a country dike. That you refuse dates from men because you prefer women. That's why you do what you do, so, um, well . . . you know, so you can look at them down there." My cheeks flushed with embarrassment. Trying to shame my own mother made me feel like filth.

"Well, seeing as how I do look at lady parts all day long I guess I can see where these *people* would confuse the two situations." She smiled at me, amused by my gumption. I knew she could see right through me.

We were both quiet for some time, deciding our next moves. Mom was the first to speak. She patted the side of the armchair, my cue to have a seat and call a truce. "I have my theories about why you like Bobby, but I will keep those to myself. The truth is that the young man scares me. He seems a lot like his father. I have never been too strict about what you can and cannot do. I feel like I have always been fair with you, Charlotte."

"I just wish you could trust my judgment," I had said.

"Sometimes when we are young our judgment is tested. When I was your age I didn't have anyone around to really look after me. Your granddaddy tried, but he just wasn't very good at it. He spent too much time missing your grandmother and looking for her at the bottom of a bourbon bottle. I made a lot of mistakes back then that sometimes I wish I could take back and I don't want the same thing to happen to you. Sometimes, I wish I hadn't waited so long to have a child of my own so all this advice wouldn't seem so damn old."

I smiled and shook my head, some of my anger fading. "You're not as old as you think. Besides, you *had* to wait so long to have your own child so you could find dad. Right?"

She never answered me. Instead, she took my hand and warned me. "Bobby is trouble. I feel it in my bones like I feel the rain coming six days before it is forecasted. I've never put restrictions on you before, but I am now. You are not to have anything to do with Bobby Cullins."

## Chapter 9 – Addie
### *1978*

Sometimes there is just no excuse for stupidity. This is what Addie told herself three months after she had tossed those silver packets into the trash at St. Roberts. Again, she found herself waiting and watching, only this time she wasn't parked in front of Sylvie's medical practice. Instead, she was parked across the street from the cemetery on Cherry Lane, watching a mother and daughter in an intimate moment. She felt ashamed, embarrassed, and deeply saddened that she was intruding, even if her presence wasn't known.

Addie couldn't see their faces, but Sylvie's hair was down, the breeze blowing it around her face. Charlotte wore a purple corduroy jumper with a white long sleeved shirt underneath; her hair was in two pigtails that reached the middle of her back. After a few minutes of standing silently together, Sylvie sat down cross-legged and took out a book. Charlotte started doing cartwheels, turning in circles, and occasionally stopping to inspect something in the grass. The ritual of grief, Addie had thought.

If she had known that she would end up across from the cemetery this afternoon, she never would have started following Sylvie that morning. Of course, if she had bothered to pay attention to the date she would have known. Addie heard another car approaching and looked in her rearview mirror. It was a red Cadillac that could only belong to Mabel Schulte. She looked down into her lap as if praying so she wouldn't be noticed. The last thing she needed was everyone knowing her business and Mabel's loose lips were usually the bearer of such news.

The Cadillac passed, parking farther up the street. Addie watched Mabel emerge from the vehicle, carrying a picnic basket in one hand and a blue and white quilt under her other arm. As she approached the mother and daughter, Charlotte saw her first and went running to her. Sylvie slowly marked the page in her book and stood up, brushing the dirt from her pants. She and Mabel briefly hugged; an odd and unusual display of affection for Sylvie who rarely put her feelings on display. The three of them then sat down in front of Martin Day's grave and ate.

It wasn't Addie's business and she shouldn't have been there, but she couldn't manage to make her hand turn the ignition and start the car. Instead, she remembered a time when she and Sylvie were on friendly terms. But that all changed when Martin died. Sylvie blamed her and Bart as well as Mabel's brother Harold for Martin's death, or at least the events leading up to his death. It had been two years since that horrible day and if Addie could take back her part in all of it she would, but she had since learned that wishing something was different holds absolutely no magic. They are wasted thoughts.

Still, her thoughts wandered right back to that place where jealousy resided deep inside her bowels. Jealousy was another wasted thought and a sin at that, but nonetheless it was there and it made Addie a person she couldn't stand to look at in the mirror. Watching Sylvie at Martin's grave, she couldn't help but wonder what that must be like, to love someone so deeply. She knew that she was capable of this love. She felt it at times with her children, but not as fully as she should. Since the day she first met Bart at that revival, the zest for life had been slowly extracted from her, leaving her a puppet and a mimic just going through the motions of life.

Too many times over the years she had replayed those moments she had first laid eyes on Bart. She remembered considering her options, questioning whether or not he was someone she wanted to be involved with. She wished she had trusted her instincts when they told her he would only cause her unbearable pain. How was she to know that loving someone like him would turn her into someone unrecognizable? But isn't everyone unrecognizable to their former selves after years and years of turning the pages on the calendar?

Addie didn't know Sylvie when she was younger, but she had heard the stories; especially the one about her father getting killed so viciously on the train tracks after an all-day binge. "Parts were scattered east, west, north and south," Bart had told her one night when he was warning her to not get messed up with that bad karma. She had wondered if Bart even knew what karma meant, because if he did he had certainly secured his role as cow dung in the next life.

What had fascinated her the most about this woman was that in spite of a father who couldn't be counted on to walk a straight line and whose mother didn't live long enough to teach her how to be a proper lady, she actually seemed to make a better life for herself. After her father had been killed on those tracks, she had just disappeared. No one knew where she had gone even though it was unlikely that too many people cared.

"Harold cared," Bart had told her one evening when Sylvie first came back to town and caused a stir. She rolled into town just after Christmas right before the New Year, 17 years older with a white coat and a stethoscope.

"Why would he care?" she had asked. The few times that she had seen him and Sylvie near each other they acted like they didn't know each other. Aside from a few obligatory words, they rarely spoke.

"I think he thought he was going to marry her." Addie must have looked stunned when he said this because Bart laughed. Oh, she had loved it when she could make him laugh instead of scowl. Too bad she didn't have a talent for comedy too often. "Don't laugh. It's true. Used to follow her around like a little puppy, but she just seemed to tolerate him. She's as strange as her old man was."

"She doesn't seem strange. Just quiet," Addie had observed. When she had married Bart and came back to live in Marion with him she didn't feel like she quite fit in with the other women in town. Even when she had Elvira and had motherhood in common with the other townies, she felt oddly dismembered from the group. When Sylvie, who was clearly so different from the other women in Marion, had sauntered into town she thought that maybe she would find a friend at last.

"Don't kid yourself, babe. That woman is the devil. Hell, she led Harold on for months and then didn't even bother to say one word to him when he was laid up in the hospital with his gimpy leg. Just up and left. Now, she comes back with her education and thinks she is going to do what?"

Addie didn't know what Sylvie's intentions were, but she thought that maybe they could strike up a conversation. Against Bart's demands she scheduled an appointment with the new doctor, with the hopes of striking up a friendship with a woman who seemed to be just as much as an outsider as herself.

What struck Addie the most when Sylvie stepped into the exam room was how beautiful she was. Not in a conventional way, but in a way that makes you reconsider what beautiful is. Her features were defined and strong, which went against her slight and almost elfish physical stature. Addie was once pretty, too, she reminisced. In fact, she had the wholesome good looks that made her more than eligible for any number of state fair beauty queen competitions, but that was before three broken noses and two split lips beat away the prettiness. Now, her looks were at the mercy of a man and natural reconstruction.

"Since opening my practice I have managed to meet quite a few of the new women in town. Well, at least the ones who weren't grown and bred from this soil. But not you. What brings you in?" Sylvie asked. She smiled at Addie with her eyes. Not just with her mouth, but her eyes. Not many people ever do that, Addie realized. Probably because smiling is a mechanical reaction that lets people go on believing that you're fine, life's dandy, nothing to worry about, so move on.

Addie ran her hands back and forth across her thighs, the paper gown feeling smooth and revealing under her hands. "Just wanted someone to talk to, I guess."

Sylvie looked perplexed. "I'm not that kind of doctor."

"What kind of doctor is that?"

Sylvie tapped her head. "A head doctor; someone who gets in there and tries to figure it all out. I prefer babies and Pap smears, those things I know. What goes on in someone's head I have no business messing with."

"I don't think that's what I need," Addie said.

"You're Bart's wife?" Sylvie asked. Addie nodded. "How's he treating you?"

"Like a husband treats his wife."

"That's a subjective assessment."

"He ain't all that bad. I actually think I am quite lucky to have landed him to be honest."

"How's that?" Sylvie asked.

Addie blushed and looked back down in her lap, tucking a strand of hair behind her ear. "He's a good man. He works hard for us. He can be tender."

"And dangerous."

Addie shrugged. "People can change."

"Hate to be the bearer of bad news, Mrs. Cullins, but Bart isn't much the changing type. You'd be better off trying to teach a bull not to use his horns or a dog not to lift his leg to a tree."

"It's hard making friends in this town. Been here nearly eight years and I still barely know anyone. Why is that?"

"Small towns aren't exactly open to strangers, plus most people around here are secretly afraid of your husband, to put it plainly. He has a reputation."

Addie frowned. "I ought to be going."

"So there's nothing I can do for you?"

Addie shook her head and stood. "I'll just get dressed and leave you to your real patients."

"All the women that walk through these doors are my patients."

"Sure. Okay." She hopped down from the table and reached for her clothes, folded neatly in an armoire in the corner. She remembered too late that the back of her gown left her exposed. She felt Sylvie's tender fingers on her cold skin, the tips running along her spine. Her spine that was mottled with bruises. Addie couldn't bring herself to turn around. Instead she had whispered, "People can change."

"For your sake I hope they can," Sylvie said. Addie stayed in the same position clutching her clothes to her chest, holding her breath until the door to the exam room shut.

***

The wheels of the Marquis bounced along the dirt path leading to the farmhouse. It was a clear night, perfect for gazing at the stars if you were fickle enough to believe in star gazing wishes. The windows were open, inviting in enough dirt to leave a fine film on the steering wheel. The radio in the Marquis only got one station. During the day it played blue grass music, but at night the banjos were silenced and the format changed to Christian talk radio. Perhaps the station managers realized that once the sun went down, hell and damnation afflicted enough people to warrant the evangelizing that poured out of the speakers.

The last time Addie had found herself on this desolate dirt path to Sylvie's house she came as a messenger of death. She wished she could have been more eloquent in her delivery, but in the end she could only utter two devastating words, "Martin's dead." It pained her more than a million blows to the back of her head to see the mask of devastation that darkened Sylvie's face. Addie had many regrets in her life, but her greatest regret may have been that instead of comforting Sylvie during her sudden grief, she had merely turned on her heel and walked away. When she had gotten back into her car, she managed for split second to look back at the house only to see Sylvie supporting herself against the doorframe, staring off into the distance as Charlotte tugged on her pants leg.

Addie wasn't sure that Sylvie would even be awake at this hour. She didn't bother to wear a watch, but she assumed it was close to midnight. After she made sure everyone was fast asleep she made her getaway. She eased the car around the back of the house, parking in the soft grass, turning the ignition off, and sat in her car listening to the sound of the engine settling under the hood. Could she do this? She didn't have a choice. Asking Sylvie for help once after the part she played in Martin's death was one thing, but to come back for seconds? That was merely pathetic.

*Rap, rap, rap.* The sound startled her, causing her to jump so violently that her thigh hit the steering wheel hard. Sylvie was standing alongside her car banging at the window, wearing a white bathrobe and men's boots. The sight made Addie want to chuckle, but really, what did she expect? Certainly she hadn't expected Sylvie to be dressed to the nines at this hour.

Sylvie stepped back to let her out of the car. "This is intolerable, Addie. What makes you think you can show up here in the middle of the night? I told you I couldn't help you."

"I know, but I need to talk to you. Please?"

Sylvie didn't budge or make any motions to indicate that Addie would be welcomed inside. "I am not your personal pharmacy. You understand that? I gave you all I could that day in my office. So you best be getting back in that car and head home."

"It's not pills that I need."

"Then what do you want?"

"I'm pregnant. I couldn't take the pills. If Bart had found out he would have … well, he would have come unhinged."

Sylvie shook her head and pulled the robe tighter across her body. "Why would you do such a thing? Those pills were meant to help you."

"How would they help me if I was lying in a hospital bed on life support? Can I come in?"

"That is not a good idea, Addie. Charlotte's asleep and I don't feel like entertaining right now. If you want to talk, call me during office hours. I will get you a referral to an obstetrician. You will have to go a few towns over, but it's the closest referral I can give you."

"You're not understanding. I'm not having this baby."

Sylvie narrowed her eyes. "What are you asking me?"

"I need services," Addie whispered.

"I don't provide those services."

"But Sylvie, you have to know that I'm asking out of desperation. I know it's wrong, but this is the choice I'm making."

"What about Bart?"

"Do you think he cares?"

"I mean what are you going to do if he ever finds out? How did you even get away from him tonight? From what you've eluded to and from what I've seen, he keeps you on a very tight leash."

"I had some pain killers from one of those times when he got too angry. A couple pills disguised in his dinner and a six pack of beer will knock anyone out."

"Or kill them."

"Whatever. I'm not too picky these days." Sylvie turned away from her. A coyote screamed in the distance, an ominous warning. But Addie wasn't letting Sylvie walk away from her. She reached out and grabbed her arm. "You can't turn me away."

"Take your hands off me," Sylvie demanded.

"Do you not have any compassion? I mean you must, because I see you with your daughter and with other people, your patients, and you seem nearly human."

Sylvie closed the difference between her and Addie, coming so close that the smell of toothpaste lingered between them. "Why do you deserve my compassion?"

"I didn't think that Bart would take it as far as he did. He just wanted to have a little fun with Marty. I swear to Jesus, I didn't know he intended to kill him. "

Sylvie raised her hand. Addie's first instinct was to duck, but she soon realized that the hand was only meant to signal silence, not violence. "I don't need or want an explanation of that morning. I know what happened. As far as my compassion? I have plenty of it. In fact, I do feel sorry for you because you seem like a person who just got stuck in a story that became a way of life."

"Then help me. Do you know someone who can do it?"

"Answer me this question. What is going to happen if you get pregnant again? You can't just keep aborting your babies."

"You let me worry about that. I have a plan. You know, Sylvie, I never thought you were a God-fearing woman. I thought this would be easier for you than me."

"One doesn't have to believe in a God to have morals and ethics. The truth is that I don't object to an abortion, Addie. You're not hearing me. I just don't see how this one act is going to solve the whole of your problems."

"I told you I have a plan."

Sylvie considered her. "How far along do you think you are?"

"I don't know. About six weeks? That's good, right? The earlier the better?"

"I wish you had other options," Sylvie said.

"Well, from personal experience I can tell you that that wish ain't coming true. I ran out of options a long time ago. Just get me an appointment and I'll take care of the rest."

"You think it's that easy?"

"Isn't it?"

"Go home and make sure that barbaric husband of yours is still breathing. The last thing you need is to kill a man."

"Sylvie, please. Another child will kill me."

"Addie, I think Bart took your life ages ago." With that, Sylvie walked into her home, leaving Addie standing in the dark, pregnant and alone. She contemplated Sylvie's last words and found that she couldn't quite disagree.

\*\*\*

It is a crooked path through life that one walks, always meeting obstacles to overcome. In another time, life could have been simpler for her. She had finally come to terms with this in the pre-dawn hours after she returned from the farmhouse. Standing at the foot of her bed, she watched Bart sleep. His chest rose heavily and fell again. For so many years Addie had managed to exist by appreciating the small blessings in her life: Bart beat her to a bloody pulp frequently, but he didn't snore. Elvira was a colicky, impossible baby, but she had eyes like an angel to compensate. Her other four children ravaged her body when they were born, Bobby nearly killing her, but they made her appreciate the hand of God a little bit more each time. For everything bad there was a sliver of good that could be discovered if she looked hard enough. But the truth was that she was tired of looking.

She went outside to the shed behind their house. The shed was littered with old lawn mower parts, broken beer bottles, and various hunting gear. She gathered two dusty green jars that smelled like turpentine and held them tight to her chest with one arm as she grabbed the can of kerosene on a shelf. Walking slowly, but with a newfound purpose, she approached the car, which she had left parked a good five hundred feet from the house. She poured kerosene in the jar and grabbed a blanket from the backseat, pausing only for a second to consider whose blanket this was before ripping it in half and stuffing the halves in each one of the jars. Her purpose was clear.

With a stick she found lying near the car she pushed the pieces of ripped blanket farther into the kerosene making sure they were soaked. When she was done she walked back into the house that she had called a home for too many years to count. She considered checking on the children, but thought better of it. What good would it do? They were asleep. They would not feel the tenderness of her kiss. It was better this way. That is how she had convinced herself. Instead she went into the kitchen and grabbed a book of matches. She paused to wash her hands to get rid of the kerosene. Then she washed her face, smoothed her hair, and took the quilt her mother had given her as a wedding gift from the back of the couch.

Addie returned to the car, curling up underneath the blanket in the backseat, waiting for the morning to awaken. Just before the autumn sun rose over the trees, Bart pulled open the car door and clumsily climbed behind the wheel. He grunted as he shifted, getting comfortable. He started to turn the ignition, but instead grumbled, "What the hell smells like skunk in here?"

In response to his question Addie pushed the quilt off of her head and sat up taller than even she thought possible. The last words she spoke to her husband as she lit the match and let those glass bottles of kerosene light up the sky with a sunrise of a different kind were, "I have a plan."

## Chapter 10 – Charlotte
### *Present*

Did I listen to my mom about staying away from Bobby Cullins? Of course I didn't. By refusing to resist the pull that Bobby had over me, I was flattening the trust between my mom and me. I was also turning into a different, unhealthy version of myself that would only get worse during – and long after – Bobby and I were a couple.

"I don't like missing school," I had told him one afternoon when we were riding along the back roads in his sister's car.

"School sure ain't missing us," he said and ran his hand along my thigh. "Besides, I can teach you things that are much more useful than integers and pronouns."

"What if school calls my mom?" I asked.

Bobby sighed, removed his hand from my thigh, and raked his fingers through his hair. "Jesus, Charlotte. So what if they do? You know how many times school has called my house? I think they just eventually stopped expecting a response."

"My mom's not like your sister," I said.

"What's that supposed to mean?" he asked.

"Nothing," I said scooting closer to the passenger door, putting distance between the anger in Bobby's voice and the feelings of inadequacy in my heart.

I had made a promise to my mom to not see Bobby. By the time

I was riding in Bobby's truck that promise was two months old and a thousand lies later. It's funny now, as I am faced with the lies of omission my mom kept from me, that I still feel enormous guilt when I think about how much pain I put her through when the truth came out. At the same time I get angry because I am left to deal with the fallout of her lies and where is she? I know that is an unfair question to ask. It makes me sound like a horrible daughter.

"No, it doesn't," Nick assures me as we lie in the double bed in my old bedroom. His delicate fingers and calloused hands caressed my arm as I lie next to him in my favorite position. People call it "spooning" and I hate that term. It sounds incredibly ridiculous and juvenile for an intimate position that makes me feel loved and protected. It seems silly that a grown woman needs to constantly feel protected, especially when I put off vibes to everyone else that I am tough and strong. The truth is I mask a lot of my feelings. I am beginning to believe it is one of the many traits that make me Sylvie Day's daughter. Then my thoughts wander to her other daughter.

"I wonder what she's like."

"Who?" Nick murmurs in a tone that makes me certain he was teetering on the edge of sleep.

"Her."

"She has a name."

"Saying her name makes it too real. I don't think I am ready for all of this to be real. Mom being gone, a sister when I've been an only child for thirty-six years. It's too much, Nick. What if she looks like Mom? That would be too much to handle right now."

Nick rolled over and rubbed his eyes. "I thought you didn't want to meet her."

"I don't. Or maybe I do. I haven't really decided yet. Harold called today to ask me if I wanted her address." I said.

"Do you?"

I rolled over onto my stomach. It was still flat enough not to cause me discomfort. "It would be good to have I suppose. He wants to meet her."

"That's understandable. This is just so incredible."

"If that's what you want to call it then okay. It's incredible; an incredible mess."

\* \* \*

That first day I played hooky from school Bobby and I went back to his place, where he lived with his oldest sister, Elvira and her two children. His other three siblings had long since moved away from Marion. Jack, the eldest boy, had joined the Navy as soon as he was eighteen and he hadn't been back since. That was nearly ten years ago, shortly after Bobby's mother had blown apart the remainder of her marriage, reducing it to mere fragments scattered in the front yard, reminding folks that love and marriage didn't always go hand in hand. Gracelyn and Johnny were twenty months apart and were both in college on scholarships two states away in the Ohio River Valley. For the most part the family had adjusted after losing both of their parents so violently.

Aside from a total lack of superstition and a tendency for inviting the odd man here and there into her bedroom, as well as growing a small patch of marijuana in her dad's old shed, it didn't appear that Elvira's presence was creating problems. Elvira had done her best to take care of her siblings and it seemed like they were all doing fine. This made me suspicious of my mother's warnings. How bad could they be? But no matter how many times I tried to broach the subject of Bobby with her, I was cut-off.

"It's not a matter we will be discussing any farther, Charlotte. That family's dysfunction is permeated in the blood line."

My mother's warning had rung like a broken bell in my head as I sat on Bobby's couch nursing the beer he had popped open for me. He lay on the couch with his feet in my lap, guzzling his third can of Stag.

"Maybe you ought to slow down," I had suggested.

Bobby responded with a disgusting burp and an insult. "You're becoming a bore, Char."

"I have to be home by seven or my mom will wonder where I am. If you're hammered, how am I getting home?"

Bobby removed his feet from my lap, took the beer I had been nursing out of my hand, and pulled me on top of him. His breath reeked of beer. To this day I cannot stand the way beer tastes or smells. Thankfully, Nick prefers bourbon and water. If he had been a beer drinker, I don't think I would have been able to fall for his good looks, charm, and a nice ass aside. It just wouldn't have been possible.

"Come on, Char. Let's have some fun. I didn't bring you here just to steal El's beer." He held the back of my head with his hand and kissed me, his teeth mashing into mine and his tongue darting in and out. The first time he had ever kissed me I thought he was the best kisser and no one could ever ignite the passion that rose inside me quite like he did. I was wrong on both accounts, but I blame youth and inexperience on those assumptions. But the way Bobby kissed me when we were lying on his couch was sloppy and completely disgusting.

"You're too drunk, Bobby. It's no fun. Your breath is rank."

"You know I could have any girl I want, right Char? So you shouldn't be so picky. What's the problem anyway? It's not like this is our first time."

He was right. We had been actively exploring each other for the past couple of weeks. It was an awkward time for me. I wasn't sure how I felt about sex. Sometimes it felt good, but the physical pleasure only lasted for a short time and what I was left with was the mental anguish of feeling less and less like the good girl I was supposed to be.

"Do you have a condom?"

Bobby quit kissing me long enough to dig around half-assed in his pockets. "Doesn't look like it. I could find a balloon. El's got those things all over because her little brats love to blow them up and sit on them. It's incredibly annoying."

"That's the dumbest idea I ever heard. We should stop."

"Why do we need to even worry about condoms? Can't you just ask your mom for the pill?"

"It doesn't work like that Bobby. One, I'm not even supposed to be looking at you, much less fucking you. Second, my mom doesn't just keep those things around the house."

Bobby wasn't going to let my protests discourage him. There were plenty of things that Bobby Cullins cared very little about, but screwing me or any of the other girls in town (as I would later find out happened quite often behind my back) wasn't one of them. Instead of hearing what I was saying, he began fumbling with the buttons on my shirt and although I wanted to vomit as his beer soaked tongue probed my mouth, I didn't tell him to stop.

Thinking back on that time, I have a million regrets. To list them all would be pointless, though, because the thing about regrets is that no matter how fervently you want to denounce them they stay with you. They are emotional parasites that refuse to be exterminated. So the only thing left to do is ignore them and go about your business as if they weren't there. That is the only way to peacefully co-exist with regret.

\*\*\*

I knew it was a bad idea to fall asleep with thoughts of Bobby Cullins in my head. Nick had to shake me several times before I would wake up from the nightmare that left me sweating profusely and my voice hoarse from screaming.

In my dream Bobby was driving me home after our tryst on the couch. My shirt was ruffled and buttoned incorrectly, while Bobby looked perfectly put together as we glided along the freshly paved road back into town. Smoking a cigarette and drinking another beer, his fifth or sixth by this time, Bobby was driving too fast and barely able to manage the steering wheel. In my dream signs keep flashing, warning drivers of fresh oil and loose gravel.

"Slow down!" I yell. The windows are rolled down, carrying my voice out of range.

He doesn't listen. He just keeps gaining speed, driving into the sun that is taking its sweet time to set. I don't have my sunglasses and I remember that I had left them in my purse, which is lying on the floor in Bobby's living room. I put my hand up to shield the sun. "Slow down!" I say again.

Bobby laughs and looks over at me. "You really are quite a kill joy aren't you?"

That's when the wheels slide on the pavement and the car begins to spin in circles. The cigarette Bobby has between his lips lands on my hand, burning my flesh, while he exclaims, "Fuck!" Three, four, five times the car spins before hitting something and becoming airborne, flipping over twice before finally coming to a stop upside down. I feel blood trickling into my ears and a sharp pain in my neck.

"Oh, my God. Oh, dear sweet Jesus. Holy fuck! Holy fuck!" These are the words that I hear coming from Bobby's mouth. I try to turn my head to make sure he is okay, but I can't move; when I try to move the pain cuts deeper. Of course, if I could see myself from afar I would know why. I would see that the reason that razor sharp sensation is rippling through my body is because there is a five-inch shard of glass from one of the windows lodged into my neck.

This is when I wake up. Nick sits me up and brings me a glass of water. He tells me over and over again that it is just a dream. While he tries to comfort me with lies, I hold the back of my neck and breathe in and out, in and out, willing myself to believe him this time. But unfortunately, we both know my dream isn't a nightmare and I have the scar on my neck to prove it.

## Chapter 11 – Harold
### *1978*

He stood in front of the farmhouse door with his hand raised, poised to strike, but he kept resisting the motion. Isabel had pushed him out the front door as soon as news had started to rumble through town of the events that had unfolded in the early morning hours out at the Cullins'.

"Please go tell Sylvie," she had urged. "She'll want to know."

"I don't think that she would care much to see me or be too affected by what happened to the Cullins. Have you forgotten? Can't I just call her?"

Isabel put her hands on her hips, narrowing her eyes at her husband. "Of course not. No, a conversation like that needs to be done face to face."

"I'm sure once she manages to get that girl of hers to school she will hear the news. It's really none of our concern, Isabel. We would just be meddling. That's my sister's job, not ours. She'll tell her."

"Margaret Lin told me a few weeks back that she saw Addie at Sylvie's office," she persisted.

"I still don't see what that has to do with anything."

"I'm just wondering if maybe she spoke to Sylvie about things."

Harold shook his head at his wife's naivety. Even though this aspect of her personality was exasperating to him at that moment, it was her pure heart that he loved so much. It made him forget about the abhorrent behavior he was capable of, while reminding him that he could be loved deeply by someone if he was willing to open his heart. It was a fine line he walked every day, wanting to be the person that deserved this woman's love and pushing away the feelings of emptiness and resentment he felt every time he walked into a courtroom or wrote a brief because he had been cheated out of the life he was supposed to live. Although he knew that his own actions had caused his life to take a different course, he still blamed Sylvie.

"I can't imagine that she would have seen Addie. She doesn't have the capacity to forgive like some people do."

"She may surprise you," Isabel suggested.

The inability to forgive and let go of the past was something that he and Sylvie shared; not something that Isabel would ever understand. Instead of acknowledging and accepting Isabel's statement, he said, "Even if Sylvie does talk to me what could she say? Their conversation is protected by patient-client confidentiality. So it's a moot point, really."

Isabel had thrown her hands up in the air then sat down at their kitchen table resigned to the fact that answers were not to be had. "I just feel so horrible for those babies. Losing both their parents like that."

"They'll probably be better off."

"How can you say such a thing?"

"Because it's true. I don't know about Addie, but everything Bart touched suffered in one way or another." Harold limped over to the kitchen sink to take his daily dose of pain relief. So many years had passed since the horrific night on the train tracks, but his damaged leg refused to let him forget. He tossed his head back and let the pills slide down his throat. Relief should come within the next several minutes. He only wished that there were pills to help him with the other chronic situations that pained him.

In the end, he let Isabel convince him to drive out to Sylvie's. He still wasn't prepared to speak to her when she answered the door. In fact, he hadn't spoken to her in two years – since Marty's funeral.

Even during the trial, if you could even call it that, she wouldn't look at him. He couldn't blame her. He couldn't even stand himself. When he walked into the courthouse restroom, he couldn't even look at himself in the mirror. If she had looked at him, her eyes would have asked, "How? How can you defend that man?" He's glad he never had to answer the question.

"Another person I don't want to see knocking on my door at some ungodly hour," she said.

"What's that mean?" Harold asked.

She didn't answer him. "I have a full schedule today, Harold. If there is something you need just get to the point."

"Fine. Addie Cullins blew her and Bart up last night. A bomb in their car."

"What?" Sylvie gave him an incredulous look. "Once again your humor is lost on me."

"Why would I come all the way out here to play a practical joke on you? Isabel thought you would like to know. That's the only reason I am even here."

"But why would she do that?" Sylvie whispered.

"I guess she was tired of waiting for Bart to finish her off."

Sylvie briefly met his gaze and for split second he thought he recognized a trace of guilt or remorse. But before he could entertain the thought any longer, she turned away from him and walked into the house, leaving the door ajar. He followed her and saw Charlotte sitting at the kitchen table eating a bowl of cereal, her hair as wild and unkempt as her mother's used to be. He looked away to push aside the memory.

"Charlotte, go upstairs and get dressed. We have to go to school." The little girl shoveled one last spoonful into her mouth and darted up the stairs.

"Is everything all right?" Harold asked.

Sylvie glanced at him as if she were surprised to find him in her presence. "You're not welcome here. Please leave."

"Come on, Sylvie. Are we going to continue to do this dance?"

"I don't dance," she said flatly. "I'm not very good at it."

Harold tried a different approach. "Isabel told me that Addie had been by to see you a while back."

"Did you change careers, Harold? Playing detective now? Tired of defending hopeless human beings who go around killing other people's husbands?" Sylvie was fiddling with a paper bag and filling it with more items from the fridge than one little girl could possibly eat.

"I know what you think of me. I was only doing my job."

"Right, because someone put a gun to your head and forced you to defend that bastard. You always were Bart's little shit, weren't you?"

The silence in the kitchen lasted for a long moment. Harold knew he should go and not press his luck any farther. He did what he had promised Isabel. But something continued to nag at him. "When you left there were rumors," he finally said.

"People talk in small towns. Doesn't mean they are worth listening to."

"Why did you leave without saying a word? All those years ago?"

"Look, Harold. I told you back then that our relationship wasn't what you wanted it to be. As for why I left, it isn't any concern of yours."

"You never did seem to care about what other people said."

"Still don't. All that I care about is building a nice life for Charlotte and I. Beyond that nothing else matters." She threw the brown bag into Charlotte's knapsack and brushed past him. He followed her back into the living room where the front door still stood wide open. Sylvie didn't seem to notice.

"When you left I never got to say I was sorry about your father." Those words stopped Sylvie in her tracks. She didn't turn to face him, but from the rise and fall of her back between her shoulder blades he could tell she was breathing heavier than usual. "I realize now he was a man who got a bad rap, just a product of so much bad luck."

Sylvie turned on him. "Really? You realize that now? Is that why all those years ago it was so easy for you to let my father take the rap for what happened out on those tracks?"

Harold felt his blood pressure rise, a cautionary reflex that happened when he was being called out. A better man would have stopped the farce right then and there. A better man would have admitted that he had fucked up all those years ago. A better man would have begged for mercy and fallen on his knees to receive his punishment. But Harold wasn't a better man. "I have no idea what you are talking about."

"I find that incredibly unbelievable."

"I don't have much recollection of that night," he insisted.

"I don't doubt it, considering you had drunk nearly a pint of bourbon before the accident. You let people believe that a man you deemed lesser than you become the laughing stock of the town once again. Instead of letting him die a hero, he died a drunk. But you know what? I know the truth."

Harold laughed. "Well if you must know the truth, you're partly to blame for your father's death just as much as I am."

Sylvie crossed her arms in front of her. "Same old Harold. Not much changes after twenty some odd years, huh? Still blaming everyone else for your mistakes."

"You cut me off, Sylvie. Like I was worthless and didn't matter to you. I loved you, faults and all. But you couldn't be bothered to love me back."

"I wasn't obligated to feel the same way about you."

Once again Harold was overwhelmed with emotions that were impossible to contain. If Isabel had known how strong his feelings were for Sylvie, she may have never suggested he come out to the farmhouse. But how would she know this? Once Sylvie had left town he suppressed those feelings. He worked hard to erase the memories of her lying in the back of his truck; bits of hay clinging to her hair; the way his fingers tingled when he ran them along her collarbone. He moved quickly towards her and said, "I loved you more than anyone could have possibly loved you."

He had pushed too hard. As he came towards Sylvie she backed away. She moved to the armoire in the corner of the room and grabbed something long and slender from the top of it. It wasn't until the barrel was under his jaw that he realized it was a shotgun. Against his better judgment, he laughed. "That thing isn't even loaded."

"You willing to take the chance?"

"Come on, Sylvie. Calm down." He felt the barrel of the gun press harder against his skin as Sylvie edged him out of the living room and onto the front porch.

"You have no right to tell me no one could love me any better than you. Once again you are making false declarations, Harold. Martin loved me. His love was something so deep and intangible that sometimes to be in the presence of it was overwhelming. He understood my pain. He was a warm wind on a cold day that wraps itself around you, making you feel protected and invincible. But once again, someone stole that love from me and you had the audacity to defend the person who did it. I'm sorry that poor woman got dragged to hell with him, but she did everyone a favor. So go home and tell your wife that. Or whatever version of the story you want to concoct." Sylvie cocked the hammer of the shotgun. "Now get off my land."

Something fell nearby. The drama of the moment was broken or heightened, depending on how you look at it, by the realization that they weren't alone. At the same time both Harold and Sylvie turned toward the noise and saw Charlotte standing in the doorway of the kitchen holding her knapsack. The apple had fallen out and was rolling on the ground. The expression on her small face made Harold's heart hurt.

He gently wrapped his fingers around the barrel, lowered the gun, and walked away.

Chapter 12 – Charlotte
*Present Day*

After a traumatic event like a car accident most people say that they don't recall much. That everything is a blank. These are the lucky ones. They don't remember the pain or the terror. They don't have images of loved ones in distress and can't recall what it felt like to be wrought with uncertainty about whether or not that person would live or die. I remember nearly every detail of the night that Bobby and I flipped his sister's car over and over again in the cornfield like it was nothing more than a Matchbox car. Oddly enough, I remember that my primary thought was, *Oh my God my mom is going to kill me.* For the longest time I worried more about getting in trouble for being with Bobby than the shard of glass protruding from my neck.

Bobby was still in the car when the paramedics arrived. Who called them, I will never know. It's not like we had cell phones back then. Only a few people were lucky enough to have actual car phones and I bet none of them were out on a country road in the middle of nowhere that evening. Nonetheless, the sirens began wailing shortly after the car came to a halt upside down. Once the men arrived on the scene, Bobby was dragged from the car. A stocky paramedic grabbed him under the armpits and yanked him free from the vehicle. I was another story.

Although I knew I was in a precarious position, I still didn't fully grasp the situation that I was in. The paramedics kept shouting back and forth to each other about the gravity of my injuries. *Don't move her*, I heard more than once. *Wait for the brace*. On the way to the hospital, I never once closed my eyes. Instead I focused on the faces of the men working on me. I watched Kevin Miller, a boy only five years older than me, furrowing his brow as he concentrated on finding a vein to start an IV. His partner, Clive Krendall, began cutting my pants off and checking for lacerations on other parts of my body. It's funny what goes through your mind when you are dangling between life and death. While these men performed their rituals designed to keep my heart pumping long enough to pass me off to the doctors and nurses at the emergency room, I was thinking about how I was going to get all the blood out of my hair. I knew it must look bad because I could feel it, sticky and matted to the back of my neck.

Just like in the movies, my mom met the ambulance at the emergency room doors and was right by my side as they wheeled me down the hall to prep me for surgery. The only time I started to feel the slightest bit fearful was when I saw the wild look in my mother's eyes as she ran alongside the gurney to the trauma room. Her pupils were dilated, there was sweat dripping from her nose, and tears were trailing down her cheeks. At that moment her bedside manner sucked. It truly scared me to see her hysterical and out of control. It had to be bad for my mother, Dr. Sylvie Day, to lose her poise during a medical situation. For that second I thought I just might be dying. After that thought, I remember feeling a needle prick and then my eyelids closed.

I spent nearly a week in the hospital after the surgery to remove the glass fragments from my neck. The surgeon had told my mom that she owed my life to Kevin and Clive. Their expert response had not only saved my life, but my ability to walk as well. "If they had moved her just the slightest bit the wrong way when getting her out of that vehicle, the situation could be a hell of a lot worse," I heard him say to my mother when they both thought I was asleep.

The week in the hospital was downright agonizing. The physical pain was under control thanks to a constant supply of narcotics, but it was the long hours I was left alone that were hardest. It was during those boring and lonely hours, I had to contemplate what came next. My mom never once mentioned Bobby or my betrayal. She seemed to be purposely avoiding the subject. Two days after the surgery, I tried to talk to her about it to say I was sorry, but she wouldn't let me get the words out. She only said, "Charlotte, we're not going to talk about that. I think that my point was proven. We are moving on."

My mother's ability to move on from things always perplexed me. While it may have been an attractive quality that many people envied (me included, when life became a lot more complicated several weeks down the road) the truth was that it annoyed me. Her insistence that some things just shouldn't or didn't need to be discussed often came off as insensitive. As an adult I would realize that this was simply denial on her part, but in those weeks after the accident, I felt a need to clear the air between us, to address the elephant in the room, so to speak. But she refused to discuss it with me.

Although she may not have wanted to discuss Bobby Cullins with me she didn't hold back her opinion with the hospital staff. When Margie Frankel, a single mother who worked the night shift and then held down a part-time job at the local gas station during the day came in to change my sheets, I asked her how Bobby was. "Did he get treated after the accident, too?"

Margie smiled apologetically at me, "I'm sorry, Charlotte. You know I can't discuss patients with you. But I can tell you that I have seen that young man in the waiting room once or twice."

"The waiting room? Why hasn't he visited me?" I asked. Even though Bobby's ignorance and lack of concern for anyone other than himself bothered me, I still couldn't believe that he wouldn't come see me. I was still clinging to some little shred of hope that he loved me like I loved him, regardless if our relationship wasn't really anything other than physical pleasure.

Margie became very quiet and turned away from me. She tugged at the corners of the bed to make the fitted sheet nice and tight. "I think that's something you should discuss with your mother."

"She won't talk to me about Bobby."

Margie sighed and looked at me. "She's just protecting her little girl." That's when I understood that Bobby had been banished to the waiting room. While my mother refused to discuss her displeasure and disappointment with me, she had no problems asserting her authority with Bobby. Later, I found out that Bobby had waited in that waiting room for nearly two days. But, in true Bobby fashion, he was easily persuaded by both my mother and his sister to leave me alone for good. At the time I felt rejection, but years later I finally understood that my mother didn't want the same fate for me as the fate that Bobby's mother had endured. She was giving me a chance to make a clean break.

***

I wish it had been that easy to make a clean break. The problem is that my mother didn't know that something else tied Bobby and I together that wasn't as easily gotten rid of. Two months after the accident I sat in Jia's bedroom, confessing my predicament.

"Are you sure?" she asked.

I shook my head as I petted her cat, Kitty Lou. Jia Lin lived on a working farm that bordered the land my parents owned. They had about a dozen farm cats that were kept around to keep the mice away, which in turn kept the snakes away from the chicken coop. All of these cats were outside cats, left to fend for themselves with the exception of a bowl of shared food each day that was delivered to them. Kitty Lou was the exception. She had been born without one eye and Jia's mother didn't have the heart to send her out there to fend for herself. Since Jia's father lived only to please his wife he happily offered sanctuary to Kitty Lou.

"I mean, I haven't taken a test or anything," I said.

"You should do that," Jia offered.

"I know."

"I can drive you. We'll tell my mom we're going for ice cream."

"Maybe," I said. "It's probably nothing. As usual I'm probably just overreacting. The accident messed up my system. That's all."

Jia leaned over the side of her bed and reached underneath. "What are you doing?" I asked.

My best friend revealed a cigar box that had been decorated with wrapping paper and glitter. "This is my rainy day fund. I keep it under here so Cai can't find it. He might be tempted to look inside, but as long as I keep this box girly and covered in glitter he'll just assume that it's a tampon box." Jia giggled at this. I thought it was humorous too but I wasn't able to muster a smile.

Jia pulled out a wad of cash. "We are going to go buy you a real pregnancy test. Not one of those dollar store tests that have been peed on, cleaned, and reused."

"That's gross. That doesn't really happen. Does it?" I always had a hard time deciphering my friend's humor.

"Look," she said, ignoring my question, "you can't very well walk into your mom's office, demanding a pregnancy test. Can you?" I shook my head. "Okay, so let's go get the test. Eat some ice cream. And then come back here and find out for sure."

"I can't go to Rite-Way to buy a test. You know how people like to talk. We'll have to go farther out of town."

After the accident, I had begun to slowly change. I became more withdrawn. I lost the ability to express myself in appropriate ways. The open relationship with my mom that had been my anchor had slowly begun to disengage. Instead of confiding in her, I absorbed my feelings. I pretended that life was just as it should be, that I wasn't seventeen years old and pregnant.

But that's exactly what the $12.99 test confirmed. Two blue lines materialized within in five seconds, fifty five seconds faster than what the instructions predicted would happen. As much as I squinted and looked at the test from different angles, I couldn't get the results to change. Jia put her arm around me, resting her head on my shoulder. She took the test from my hand, wrapped it in toilet paper, and buried it in the bottom of the trashcan.

"What's next?" Jia asked.

"I haven't the slightest clue," I confessed.

"Your mom's pretty cool. I mean mine would have the priest down here performing last rites before she killed me, but not your mom. You should talk to her."

There were lots of things I should have done that I didn't do when I was seventeen. I should have told Bobby no that night at his place. I should have talked to my mom, but I couldn't bring myself to face her and confess my sins, shattering the image she had of me. When I think back to that time, it is a little easier to understand why my mom didn't tell me about her other daughter.

Other daughter. That is a phrase I don't think I will ever get used to. It's surreal and it makes me feel uneasy about life in a way that I hadn't felt in years. Since before meeting Nick, actually. But, as I recall, wanting to please someone and to be the person they want you to be is a stronger drug than the truth. It makes you do ridiculously crazy things that eventually you will regret, but you can't be bothered to think about in that moment.

## Chapter 13 – Harold
### *1978*

After visiting Sylvie, Harold didn't drive back home. He didn't call Isabel. There wasn't really any point. Sylvie had treated him exactly as he'd expected, and given him nothing that would nourish his wife's appetite for information. Ah, Isabel, she was such a good person, Harold thought. He often found himself wondering just how in the hell he ended up married to her. It wasn't as if he was repulsive, but his personal opinion of himself just didn't quite match what Isabel thought of him or the type of person that she was. It completely baffled him that she found him sweet, charming, and worthy of her love.

On their wedding day years earlier, Mabel pulled him aside and warned him. "You be good to that woman," she said. "She is a lovely soul. The sister I never had because I got stuck with you. If you screw this up I will never forgive you." Mabel winked at her brother, gave him a peck on the cheek, and then took off to figure out why one of the twin boys was crying.

They didn't have a big wedding, which made Harold happy because he hated being put on the spot. "All I need is you and a preacher," Isabel had said. But in the end they still had family to appease so they had a small church wedding with a reception in the basement of the rectory. There were approximately fifty people in attendance. Most were friends of his and Isabel's parents, but there were also a few work associates and a smattering of nieces, nephews, and cousins.

Harold met Isabel during his second year of law school. He had been pulling an all-nighter at a bar two blocks from his residence hall. He found the commotion of the bar easier to deal with than the erratic snoring of his roommate, Lloyd Barker. The man was six foot three and weighed nearly 400 pounds. He took up so much space in the dormitory room that it was a good thing Harold was paper thin. Although Harold knew Lloyd needed to lose a couple of hundred pounds, what he didn't know was that five years later, he would be standing in a courtroom, literally giving the closing of his life. He would be standing there, looking the jury in the eye and as he demanded a conviction, putting the final nail in the coffin of the defendant's case, he would raise his hand to his chest and fall over the railing into juror number 9's lap. Dead on the spot. But the night Harold met Isabel, Lloyd slept soundly and loudly, forcing Harold to seek refuge in contract law and a glass of whiskey.

By four am when Harold couldn't keep his eyes open any longer, he began packing his books away in his leather case that was emblazed with his moniker and soon-to-be profession, Harold Klein, Jr. – Attorney at Law. It was a present from his father when he was accepted to Saint Louis University's Law School. "A little presumptuous, don't you think?" Harold had asked.

His father slapped him hard on the back, grinning from ear to ear. "I have faith in you, son."

Practicing law was not what Harold ever imagined himself doing. He still found himself clinging to old dreams. During the spring when the baseball season would begin, he would often purchase a single ticket and take in a Cardinals game at Busch Stadium. Who would have ever thought he'd have become a Cards fan? He was going to play for the Browns, but they had left town just like Baker said they would and he was stuck here with a single ticket, a hot dog, a cold beer, and a penchant for being too melancholy when sitting behind right field.

After coming to terms with his damaged leg, it was decided that he would follow in his father's footsteps. Head off to the big city, get a fancy law degree, and trudge back to that tiny Midwest town in the middle of cornfields and haystacks to work with his father. "It'll be your practice someday, son. A legacy I am proud to pass on to you."

Some legacy, Harold thought. There wasn't much in Marion that would make him famous, especially if that meant overseeing wills, mediating land disputes, and occasionally defending drunken bastards that went at each other after they drank their paychecks away at Millie's. He couldn't possibly know during this second year of law school that someday he would create a legacy, one that would haunt him and pull him farther away from himself than he ever thought possible. But at four in the morning he simply gathered up his books, slammed back the last drops of his third whiskey, and shuffled out of the bar.

He saw her sitting on a bench with her legs crossed at the ankles, her hands folded in her lap looking straight ahead. She was beautiful; ringlets of hair falling around her face and shoulders, bright blue eyes, and smooth skin. He rubbed his eyes to make sure he wasn't imagining things. He knew that sometimes three whiskeys could make his vision a little blurry and mess with his reality. But when he blinked she was still there and she was looking straight at him.

"When's the trolley come?" she asked.

"The trolley?" he questioned.

"Yes," she said patiently. "The trolley."

"You'll be waiting a long while. The trolley don't come through here no more. The autobus does, though. Although not for another couple of hours."

She had looked perplexed. "Oh, well, I don't know what to do."

"Where are you going?" he'd asked. "It's early. Streets aren't too safe so early in the morning for a woman," he said.

She raised her eyebrows at him and shook her head. "I'll be just fine. My daddy taught me well. He made sure I knew how to use bug spray and a knife when I came to this city." She patted her handbag.

"Got them both in here, want to see?"

Harold had shaken his head and took a step back. "Where you headed?"

"To my aunt's. She lives on Achtison."

"That's several blocks from here."

The woman laughed. "Which is why I was waiting for the streetcar. My aunt gave me explicit instructions how to get to her house, but she's senile. So I guess that makes me the fool for listening to her, huh?"

"I can walk you," Harold suggested.

The woman looked him up and down, and then asked. "Are you a killer? You know, like one of those guys in the Hitchcock movies?"

"No. Are you? It seems you have more weapons than me. I only have books and a gimpy leg. You seem to have a lot more at your disposal."

She laughed, throwing her head back and making her curls bounce. "I suppose you have a point. I'd like the company if you're offering. It's been a long time since I've been back to this town and I'm likely to get even more lost."

It was during that stroll in the wee hours of the early morning that Harold learned the name of his future wife, Isabel Abers. She was from Pittsburgh and had just finished school to become a nurse. Her aunt had been diagnosed as senile several months ago and her parents had begged her to come to St. Louis for a spell to look after her until they could find a way to get her in a home for the mentally incapacitated.

"It's really quite sad," Isabel had said during their walk. "She used to be such a vibrant person. We would come here to visit her and my uncle during the holidays. She would reenact the holiday party scene from *Meet Me in St. Louis* because she thought it was the most glorious movie ever made. Back then she fancied herself to be as talented as Judy Garland, which she probably was. Now, she simply forgets who she is sometimes and will introduce herself as Judy to strangers. How sad is that?"

"Does she know what's happening?" Harold asked.

Isabel smiled, sadly. "I don't think so. You know what? She actually seems happy. It's the rest of us that are so sad. Maybe we should just let her enjoy the life she's living, you know?"

"How long will you be here?" Harold inquired when they had finally made it to the house on Atchison.

Isabel shrugged. "A couple of weeks for sure, but I really don't know. Would you like to meet again for coffee sometime?"

Harold had nodded eagerly, unable to get the words to form on his tongue.

Isabel smiled, displaying brilliant white teeth that looked like they belonged to a woman of privilege. "Okay, then." She reached into her handbag then sheepishly smiled up at Harold. "Don't worry, just reaching for a pen and paper." She scribbled numbers on the scrap of paper and handed it to him. "Here's my aunt's number. Just ring me. Bye, Harold. I hope to hear from you soon."

***

Before heading home to Isabel, he drove out to the Cullins'. Where his wife had been flabbergasted that Addie had left her children alone, Harold was simply baffled that Addie had the courage to stand up to Bart once and for all because the truth was that nobody ever stood up to that man. He had to see for himself.

Like most homes in Marion, the Cullins' property was in the middle of nowhere. There weren't too many houses around, which was a blessing because the crater that had been left by the blast was evidence enough that the explosion had been bad. Harold started to get out of his car and walk over to the deputies from the sheriff's department that were standing around. He figured he could get enough information from these gentlemen to satisfy his wife's curiosity, but he never opened his car door. Instead, he sat in his car and watched two other deputies emerge from the home with the three younger kids. The oldest was leaning against the side of the house smoking a cigarette and running her hands through her hair over and over.

He and Isabel had tried for years to have children, but they were never successful. They hadn't even really been teased with false pregnancies or miscarriages. There just wasn't anything.

"I am as empty as a hollow cave," Isabel had said one night as they lay together in bed. Trying had started to get exhausting, both physically and emotionally.

"Maybe it isn't you. Maybe it's me." Harold had suggested.

"I think I am done," she said.

Harold had rolled over on his side and wrapped her curls around his finger. "We can get help." As much as he hated to say her name, he suggested, "We could see Sylvie."

Isabel had turned to him and smiled. "I don't think that's a good idea. Besides, I think it's okay to be done. We have nieces and nephews. We have each other. It's okay. Let's just be done."

Harold felt like he should try to persuade Isabel, but he refrained. First, he knew that he wouldn't be able to change her mind. Once it was set it was set. Secondly, he didn't want to push his luck. He felt guilty about his feelings, but the truth was he had never wanted kids. Isabel thought he was as ready to start a family as she was, but he couldn't fathom the thought of being a father. He didn't have the patience to relate to kids. Mabel's brood, all six of them, would sometimes come by the house on Sundays and he couldn't take it. The noise, the incessant whining; it was enough to drive someone mad. He usually begged off after a half hour, heading into town on the premise that he was working when instead he went to the office, put his feet up on his desk, smoked a cigar, and read the latest legal journals.

Watching the children being taken from their home did make him apprehensive. He wondered what would become of them. He secretly hoped Isabel wouldn't suggest taking them in because he could never say no to her. But it would be in her nature to insist that the children come stay with them. Thankfully, the oldest girl looked like she would make a good enough (at least according to her age) guardian and he wouldn't have to worry about that. He continued to watch for a little longer until he realized that it must look odd that he was sitting in his car staring. Bart had caused him enough trouble on earth, he didn't need him conjuring any trouble from down below. It was time to go home.

## Chapter 14 – Charlotte
*Present Day*

Of course I had never imagined myself being pregnant at seventeen. The only girls I had ever known who had gotten knocked up that young were uneducated, promiscuous, and unpromising. I had plans and I had promise. I had an acceptance letter sitting on the kitchen table to the University of Illinois-Chicago. That letter was my ticket away from the endless monotony of country life. Although I had been contemplating staying behind for Bobby that had all changed after the car accident; nothing was going to keep me in this place any longer than necessary. I knew exactly what I needed to do.

"What's PN?" I asked Jia. We were sitting in the cafeteria with our heads together at school contemplating my dilemma.

"Parental notification. You have to have your mom's permission because you are a minor."

"Are you kidding me?"

"Could you ask her?"

"Seriously? No, I can't ask her. It's crappy enough that I'm knocked up, but now I have to get consent to have an abortion. I thought we were living in modern times."

"Maybe Elvira can pretend to be your mom and consent for you," Jia suggested.

I pushed the tray of food away from me. Lately, food didn't taste as good as it used to. I hadn't thrown up yet, but I had a feeling that it could happen at any moment. "That is not going to happen. Bobby is not going to know about this."

"You're kind of out of options," Jia reminded me.

"Not entirely," I replied.

When I think back to all those years ago I still cannot believe how quickly everything spiraled out of control. It is a slippery slope from losing your balance to full-fledged tumbling down the hill. It happens in a blink of the eye, especially when desperation takes hold of your wrist and gives you a pull. It was desperation that guided me out of the house after my mom had gone to sleep. I ran all the way to the end of the road to meet Jia. It had taken me nearly twenty minutes and I was out of breath when I hopped in the passenger's seat.

"This is a bad idea," Jia warned.

I refused to look at her. "Just drive."

I instructed Jia to drop me off in front of my mother's practice and to drive around town a few times. "It shouldn't take long. I know where she keeps most things."

Jia started to object, but stopped when it was clear there wasn't any way she would change my mind. "Fine, but hurry up. If my mom finds out I took her car you won't see me until our college graduation."

I pulled the silver key out of my pants pocket, took a couple glances around to make sure no one was lurking in the shadows, and entered the waiting room. I didn't linger. It was best to get what I came for and go. If I gave myself too much time to think I wouldn't complete the task. I had to complete the task.

The same key that opened the front door got me into the supply closet. It wasn't customary for my mom to keep a lot of pharmaceuticals in the office. "It encourages bad habits and thieves," she used to say. She knew what she was talking about.

The drug I was looking for was intended to induce labor, but I also knew it could cause miscarriages if taken in the right dosage. How did I know this? Well, you learn a lot when medical journals are the only thing floating around in the house. This was my last chance to end the pregnancy. I had already tried all the other methods that were supposed to work, but only ended up causing me a lot of pain and grief. I had taken a meat tenderizer and slammed it over and over into my stomach only to be left with bruises and a body that was still pregnant. The next attempt was to drink a gallon of orange juice because I read that Vitamin C could cause miscarriages, but all it did was give me a horrible case of indigestion. There was always the hanger method that I had read about in books, but that seemed too brutal; not that any of the other techniques I had tried were any gentler.

I found the drug I was looking for and sprinkled a handful of pills into my palm. Better to get it taken care of the first time, I thought. To this day I am still amazed at the bravery and stupidity of that night. Irrational choices usually come from irrational fears held in place by ignorance. Jia was wrong. I had options, but I couldn't see any other option than swallowing that handful of pills and going home to wait for them to take effect. I had false hope that morning would bring a brighter future.

Nothing happened at first. I thought I hadn't taken enough. *I should have brought those pills home with me*, I thought. But I didn't know how often my mom took inventory and I didn't want her to notice a hole in her expertly organized system. I came down for breakfast and winced a little when I sat down in the chair.

"Everything okay, Charlotte?" Mom had asked.

I reached across the table for the cereal box, taking a deep breath. "Just hunger pains."

My mom sat down across from me. "We haven't talked a lot lately. You seem to be healing physically from your accident, but how do you feel up here?" She tapped her head.

"It's good, Mom. Really. I just want to forget about everything."

"Sometimes forgetting isn't best, Charlotte."

To distract her I said, "Do you think about Dad often?"

"All the time. Bad things happen and forgetting seems like the right thing to do. But if we remember we don't make the same mistakes."

"What mistakes did you make?" I asked.

"We all have our faults and it is those faults that tend to lead us into trouble."

Would my mother have opened up to me about her other daughter at that moment if I had pressed? If I hadn't brushed her advice aside? Probably not. "Like I said, everything is fine."

She sighed, her way of accepting my lame answer. "Okay, honey. Then let's get going."

On the way to school I continued to feel intermittent pain in my lower abdomen. When the pains struck I would bite down on my lip so hard that I could taste blood. All I knew is that I had to get out of the car as soon as possible or I wouldn't be able to keep up the act any longer. "I need to stop by my office for a sec, Charlotte. I left some papers I need for a meeting at the hospital this morning. Do you mind? You won't be late."

When we pulled up in front of the building, the pain had intensified. I also had the urge to go to the bathroom and throw up at the same time. "Can I come in with you and use the bathroom?" I asked.

When I lowered myself onto the toilet seat, blood gushed between my legs, while I vomited in my lap simultaneously. I thought that the violent expulsions would weaken the pain, but I was wrong. It only made the pain worse and I started to convulse. I fell off the toilet and crawled over to the door, banging as hard as I had the strength to do. When my mom found me I was laying on my stomach with my pants around my ankles, vomit trickling from the sides of my mouth.

"What the hell!" my mother exclaimed when she saw me. She grabbed me up into her lap and checked my pupils. "Charlotte, tell me what's wrong. What hurts? Did you take something?"

I nodded. "What?" she asked.

I tried to speak, but the convulsions were making me bite my tongue and I couldn't form the words correctly. "Baby," was all I could manage.

"Baby?" mom had muttered. Then in a more urgent manner, she said. "Baby! Are you pregnant?"

Again I nodded. Again, she led me. "You took something? To get rid of the baby?"

"Yes," my voice sounded faint and distant. "Here," I said.

"You took something from my office?"

"Yes."

At this point she realized the gravity of the situation and I did, too. Left without any other options, I laid on the bathroom floor of my mother's medical practice, while she completed the abortion to save my life. My memories of those moments in the bathroom are vague, but what is clear is that as my mother was saving my life, she was ending her grandchild's, and for the first time ever I saw her as something other than my mom. I saw her as a broken woman.

## Chapter 15-Charlotte
*Present Day*

Nick brought me breakfast in bed that consisted of little more than burnt toast and a scrambled egg. "We can go out for breakfast if you prefer. There really isn't anything left in the fridge unless you want tuna casserole, lasagna, or chicken noodle soup. Those we have plenty of."

I smiled at his goofy bed head and his tired eyes. Apparently, he hadn't slept well after I had woken him up. "It's okay. I'm not hungry anyway."

"How are you feeling? Is the baby okay?"

I nodded. "I think everything is fine. I'm feeling good. Sorry about all the drama last night."

Nick sat on the edge of the bed and started picking off the burnt edges of the toast. "You don't have to apologize. It's been a stressful couple of days."

"I think I want to meet her."

"Okay. If you feel up to it. We'll go after the baby is born. Where did you say she lived?"

I shook my head. "Florida. But no, I mean I want to meet her now. I know you want me to reduce the stress, but if I don't do this now I don't think I ever will."

Nick ran his hand through his hair then reached out to touch my hand. This was his preemptive move to signal disagreement in a conversation. Normally, it worked. I didn't like conflict and drama. Besides, most of the time my husband was not unreasonable when he objected to something. But this time I knew I wasn't going to give in.

"Florida? That's a long way, Charlotte. You know you can't fly and I have to be back at the office at the end of the week. The Granger's deposition for their liability lawsuit has already had to be rescheduled twice."

I pulled my hand from his and touched his face. "I'll go alone. You can fly back and I'll take the car. I have lots of free time," I joked. Since becoming pregnant I had quit my job to reduce the stress and ensure that this pregnancy stayed viable and healthy for the full nine months.

"Alone? I don't think that's a good idea."

"Well, I won't exactly be alone."

"Harold?"

I glanced away from Nick and nodded. "I told you he wants to meet her."

Nick stood up and started pacing. "It's not a good idea, Charlie."

I waved him off and picked at the burnt crumbs on the plate. Those actually looked good. Was this going to be a weird pregnancy craving I would pick up – burnt food? "Nick, he's an old man. What's going to happen?"

"He'll get you worked up. Do you remember how he acted in your mother's office?"

"He was upset. I was, too. Everyone has been upset. Besides it will give me time to get some answers."

"From him?" Nick laughed. "You have to be kidding. Answers about what?"

I shrugged. "I don't know. I'm just starting to realize that maybe he has the answers to things that I was always left in the dark about. Like my dad's death. Mom would never talk about it, but I always got the impression that other people knew. I never thought that was fair. It wasn't fair that I didn't have a father to walk me down the aisle at our wedding or to attend father-daughter softball picnics with when I was in junior high. I was jealous that other people knew what happened, but she wouldn't tell me."

"Maybe they were just trying to protect you from feeling pain. You were so young when your dad died. Do you even remember him?"

"Snippets of him. If I hadn't seen pictures I wouldn't be able to form an image in my head. That's beside the point anyway, Nick. I need to go to Florida and meet this woman. I need to not feel like an orphan."

"You have me, my parents, and this baby. You are not an orphan."

"I appreciate what you're trying to say, Nick. But even you know that's not the same."

He sat on the bed and rested his elbows on his knees. "You'll be safe, right? No chances. If it gets to be too much, pull over, dump the old man at a nursing home, and call me." I laughed. "I'm not kidding," Nick said.

I hugged him hard and gave him a peck on the cheek. "It's going to be fine, Nick. Trust me."

# Part Three

*"Life is a series of natural and spontaneous changes. Don't resist them; that only creates sorrow. Let reality be reality. Let things flow naturally forward in whatever way they like."*
— Lao Tzu

## Chapter 16 – Charlotte
### *Present Day*

When I pulled up to Harold's house he was waiting on the front porch with a cigar in one hand and a rolling suitcase in the other. Smoke curls formed perfectly as he exhaled. Although my windows were rolled up, when I closed my eyes I could still recall the sweetness of the cigars that my grandfather had smoked. "Granddaddy," I had said one Saturday morning when my mom had left me in my grandparents' care. "Did my daddy like cicars, too?"

Granddad laughed. He pretended to catch my nose and corrected me. "They are cigars, dear."

"Okay. Well, did my daddy like *cigars*, too?" Instead of an answer, I got a pat on the head, a kiss on the cheek, and an instruction to go watch some Saturday morning cartoons. Yes, Nick didn't know what it was like to always be ignored and redirected. It wasn't going to happen this time.

Harold tapped his cane against my glass. I rolled down the window. "Wake up! I might be old, but I still want to live. If you're too tired to drive, move over."

"I'm fine, Mr. Klein. Just put your bag in the trunk." I watched him shuffle alongside the car and considered helping, but decided just this once I wasn't going to practice good manners. I had a feeling you couldn't kill this man with kindness anyway. God, I hoped this woman in Florida wasn't anything like him.

Harold climbed into the passenger's seat and I smiled at him. He stared expressionlessly back at me. Did I expect him to thank me for driving him nearly a thousand miles? I guess I did.

"What? I ain't getting any younger dear. Let's go."

I sighed and started the engine, already regretting that I hadn't let Nick talk me out of this. I didn't quite know what to say, so I stuck with the usual suspects. "Hope the weather is nice down there."

"Florida is for pansies."

"Excuse me?"

Harold exhaled and stale coffee breath invaded the small space. My olfactory senses always peeked when I was pregnant; emphasizing the worst smells more than the pleasant ones. "Too many people walking around in those flowered shirts or, worse than that, old geezers wearing those too tiny bathing suits thinking they look like hot shit when really they look like elephants with saggy, baggy knees. And those pink, plastic flamingoes, well I have nothing to say about those."

Unlikely, I thought. But instead, I asked, "Have you been before?"

"I just said Florida is for pansies. Why on Earth would I have a reason to go?"

"I have been to Florida a few times and have always found the coastal areas to be beautiful."

"To each their own," Harold replied.

Indeed, I thought. I glanced over at Harold and noticed he was wearing a very formal suit. It looked like the one that he had worn the last two times I had seen him. "Is that your traveling suit?" I asked.

He looked out the window, but left his hands on his thighs. His fingers clapped onto his knees. "It's just a suit," he responded.

"When did you find out that mom had given up your baby for adoption?" I boldly asked.

Harold kept looking out the window at the watching the farmland whir by. "Are you going to talk the whole time?"

"Well, it is close to 1300 miles from here to Boca Raton. I figured conversation was a given. Why do you think she did it? You know, didn't tell you."

"How am I supposed to know the answer to that question?"

"I thought maybe she had explained herself to you when she told you about the adoption."

"Your mother never felt the need to explain nothing to anyone."

He had a point. My mom was her own person. She never felt it mattered what anyone else thought, which was both a blessing and a curse in their own right. "You didn't like her very much, did you?"

"Quite the opposite. I cared very much for your mother, but she was a hard person to love."

"I loved her. My dad loved her. Did you see all the people that came for her funeral? If that's not love then I don't know what is."

"Look, I know you have questions. But I don't think you are going to get the answers you want from me."

"If not from you, then who? The one person who could answer them is dead."

"Your mother and I hadn't talked really since before she left town to have that baby and go to medical school. I really don't have any answers. I can tell you stories, but —"

"Then tell me stories," I interrupted.

"Stories? What kind of stories?"

"Any kind. We have a long drive ahead of us and I like stories."

"Even those with an unhappy ending?"

I sighed. "Yes, even those with unhappy endings."

## Chapter 17 – Harold
*1970*

When Sylvie returned to Marion it was 1970 and Harold was sitting in Millie's, throwing back shots of whiskey on a Wednesday night. It wasn't customary for him to spend time on the bar stool, but it had been a week of monotony, representing the same type of client over and over; traffic violations and other misdemeanors that usually resulted from throwing back too much whiskey – just like Harold was doing. The citations he took care of for his clients were brain-numbing.

"Any idiot could do this," he had told Isabel countless times. Her usual response was, "Well, at least you're an idiot with a degree. That must make you a higher class of idiot, right?" He wasn't always sure it did.

That evening Isabel was hosting a book club and had shooed him out of the house practically the moment he stepped over the threshold. "No sir, mister," she had said. "I already see the grumpiness in you. I don't want your bad mood spoiling my book club meeting. This one is going to be a good one. We are discussing *Valley of the Dolls*. I can't believe it took me this long to read it."

"Dolls?" Harold had questioned.

"Go have a drink or two, maybe even three at Millie's, won't you dear? It looks like you had a hard day. The walk will do you good, too." She winked at him and patted his belly.

He was on his fifth or sixth shot (what would Isabel think?) when he heard a raspy voice ask, "Why doesn't this surprise me?"

The voice sounded familiar, but the whiskey had begun to numb his senses. He couldn't be sure he wasn't imagining it. "Sylvie?"

"Harold, is this what you have been doing for the past seventeen years? Getting drunk on a Wednesday night?"

She looked different. Older, obviously, but her shoulders were no longer rounded as if she were afraid to be seen. She sat up tall, dignified. Her clothes weren't ratty or tattered like they had been all those years ago. The only thing that was instantly recognizable was her disheveled hair. It was the hair that had kept her wild and untamable.

Rumors had circulated for a while after Sylvie had left, but as happens in most small towns, something else grabs the attention of the masses and they forget that they cared about that wisp of a girl. But Harold hadn't forgotten. He had always wondered what happened to her, always fearing the worst; but now, as she sat beside him on a wobbly barstool he wondered if he was more fearful of her return.

"What are you doing here?" he asked.

"I'm famished."

Harold shook his head. "No. I mean here. Marion. Where have you been all these years?"

"I'm moving back."

"Why?"

"Why not? I thought you would have heard. Doesn't everyone still talk in this place? They certainly did when my Dad was alive. That man couldn't take a leak without everyone knowing."

"If they talk, I don't listen. I've never been much of people person."

"Yet you're a lawyer."

"How did you know?"

"I listen. And," she nodded towards my hand, "you're married. How'd that happen?"

Harold motioned to the bartender to bring him one more ounce of liquid courage before he answered. "What's with the small talk? You don't do small talk."

"What have they said about me since I've been gone?" Sylvie asked.

"Do you care?"

She shrugged. "Not really, but it's nice to know what I'm up against. I'm renting the office space across from the post office. Setting up my own practice and I'm hoping that I will have plenty of women willing to overlook my family's history for the convenience of having an obstetrician in town. I've only been here a couple of days, but I see your population is on the verge of booming; a lot of pregnant women in this town."

"You're a doctor?"

"It's funny, huh? I bet you never saw that one coming. Bet everyone thought I left barefoot and pregnant, right?"

Harold shrugged. "Something like that."

Sylvie nodded. "Yes, that's what I thought. Well, I guess I proved all of you wrong."

She looked him dead in the eyes and walked out the door.

## Chapter 18 – Charlotte
*Present Day*

"Do you hate my mom?" Charlotte asked after Harold finished his story.

"I've never hated your mother. I just didn't understand her."

"But she kept you away from your daughter."

"Some things are not black and white. Life would have been very different for both of us if she had stayed. Was I angry when she told me? Yes, but not for the reasons you think."

"Then for what?"

"I was angry because I felt like a fool. When one feels foolish their reactions are rarely constructive. Besides, I never wanted children. Still don't, if we're being honest."

Charlotte frowned at him. "Then why are you going to see her? Don't you think you ought to go because you want a relationship with her? Are you just going to tease her? Dangle your presence in front of her face like a carrot and then walk away? What about her children, your grandchildren?"

Harold pinched the bridge of his nose and counted to ten. "Maybe she doesn't want a relationship with us. Have you thought about that? I just want to see her. I want to know if she looks like me. I want to know if she looks like Sylvie."

Charlotte didn't say anything. She kept her eyes on the road in front of her. "Does that bother you?" he asked.

"What? That you're a jackass? Yeah, kind of."

Harold laughed. "That my dear, I am. It's something that I am quite gifted at, I'm sorry to say."

\*\*\*

I wanted to try and drive another hundred miles before stopping to eat, but the lines on the road had started to blur and my stomach had been rumbling for an hour. If I didn't find something to eat soon, I would be reduced to scrounging around in my bra for crumbs from the granola bar I had eaten three hours earlier. Unfortunately, on this stretch of 24 just outside of Chattanooga there weren't too many restaurant choices, which is how we ended up at the Truck Stop, Dive Stop.

"Is this okay?" I asked.

"When you get to be my age most food tastes like motor oil anyway. This is as good a place as any, "Harold said.

"Good," I said and didn't bother to wait for him. I needed just a small break away from him, even if that meant no more than two minutes. The past several hours in the car had been exhausting. Instead of getting more comfortable, the ride continued to get tenser. Harold became more withdrawn and highly irritable. I really wished I could have a drink to take off the edge because I was truly afraid that I would hurt that old man if he crossed me one more time.

The waitress seated us at a table near the entertainment room, where smoky fumes tumbled out as the truck drivers, mostly men but some women too, played video games, chatted loudly, and occasionally let out vulgar belches. "Do you have a non-smoking section?" I asked the waitress.

The waitress popped her gum and said, "Yeah, over there." She pointed to the entertainment room. I got the point.

"I see," I said. I had considered leaving even though Harold had just managed to slide into the booth, out of breath from walking a mere 25 feet. But then I smelled the greasy food coming from the kitchen and I was seduced. In places like Disney World they actually have fans that blow the smell of the confection shops out onto the walkways so that guests will be drawn into the shops. As nasty as the truck stop was, with its questionable patrons and sticky menus, they must have known that they could always lure you into their booths with the smell of greasy food, just like Disney World.

"So, what can I get you and your old man?" the waitress asked, smiling and eyeing my Michael Kors wallet I had left sitting on the table. *This one will tip big*, is what I could imagine her thinking. I moved the wallet to my lap.

"He's not my father." "She's not my kid." We said simultaneously.

The waitress shrugged. "Whatever. I don't judge. We get all types through here."

"Just give us a minute, please." I said.

If the smokiness and the rowdiness of the truck stop bothered Harold, he didn't show it. He studied the menu, tapping his fingers on the table. His reading glasses were slipping down his nose. I noticed a piece of tape held one of the sides together. Is this what it looked like to be old, I wondered. My mom had been old, but I guess I never noticed. Sliding into oldness just seemed to be a concept that I couldn't grasp. My mom would have told me that was a luxury of being young and to enjoy it because it was quite fleeting.

Besides a few lines around my eyes where the sun had not been too kind, I still looked like I did twenty years ago. So when would it happen? Would I suddenly wake up one day and my hair would be laced with so much silver that going to the salon was pointless? Would I be walking by a store window one day, turn to admire my image, and be bitch slapped in the face with a slackened jaw and hunched shoulders? Or would it be gradual? So gradual in fact, that I would feel foolish and embarrassed that I didn't notice the change until I was looking at pictures with my grandkids one day and they would say, "Mama, you used to be so pretty."

The waitress returned, interrupting my vain thoughts. Because that is what they were, really, right? I could control many things in my life, but growing old and dying wasn't one of them. So it's best not to worry about it. Or as my mom would say, "There's no sense in ruminating over things that we have no say in. So it's best to just let it go."

Because I was starving, because I was eating for two, and because I didn't know when we would stop again, I ordered enough food to fill the stomachs of a high school football team. Two stacks of pancakes, four eggs, five sausage links, hash browns, and biscuits and gravy. Harold ordered toast and eggs. To say I felt gluttonous would be an understatement.

While we waited for our food to be brought to the table, I started to sweat profusely. This pregnancy had been relatively symptom-free except for the sporadic hot flashes. My doctor had assured me that this was a normal reaction to the fluctuating hormones brought on by pregnancy. It still didn't make it any less cumbersome. I pushed up the sleeves of my shirt, instantly regretting the decision when Harold's gaze lingered on the artwork that trailed up my left arm.

Our waitress returned with our food, slamming them down in front of us without care or ease. If she thought Michael Kors guaranteed her a tip regardless of service, she was sorely mistaken. "Nice tats," she said. Okay, maybe she'd get a better tip.

Harold gingerly stabbed his eggs with his fork and shook his head. "Tattoos. Everyone has them. They are nothing more than the mark of low intelligence and a waste of money. You could buy a box of magic markers and draw on yourself every day, which would make you slightly smarter than the average person who puts ink into their skin."

I glared at Harold. "I don't recall asking for your opinion in the matter."

"What did your mother think of about that? I assume she had some sense after all."

"She didn't discourage it."

"Figures," Harold said. He went back to eating and I decided to let the argument dissipate as I doused my first stack of pancakes in maple syrup.

Sometimes I felt self-conscious about displaying the artwork that trailed up my arm from the bend in my wrist to the crook of my elbow. The first time Nick saw this bold display of color and design imprinted onto my flesh, I thought he would be turned off. He wasn't like the other guys I had dated when I went off to college and slowly started to build a new life. He was simple, pure, the kind of guy that you want to bring home to your parents. Instead of being repelled, he whistled low and said, "That is some serious commitment. I like a woman who knows what she wants."

For the most part, my tattoo-laced arm was barely noticeable by people. This was because Harold was correct. Tattoos were commonplace. They didn't make you stand out in a crowd like they did years ago or like they would in a small farming community like Marion. But that didn't make me any less self-conscious about mine. It didn't stop me from standing in the sweltering August heat at my mother's funeral wearing a much too warm cardigan over my dress. In a big city like Chicago, no one cares. Back home, everyone would talk. The truth is that I would have preferred to have left that area of my body as unmarked and pure as the rest of my skin, but the artwork was better than the alternative.

The first time I spent the night with Nick he had laid beside me tracing the coils and curves of the Celtic design. Over and over again, his finger traced the word "brave" that was expertly incorporated into the design. Being a tattoo-virgin, he marveled at the ridges that his fingers found underneath the ink. "It's almost like it's 3-D. I didn't know tattoos could have texture," he said innocently enough.

I traced the ridges with him, my finger lingering behind his. "They usually don't."

This led me to explain to Nick the motivation behind the

tattoo. It was a tattoo designed to cover a shameful secret — a past that I wanted to run from, but stuck with me like my shadow. Of course, I had no one to blame but myself. For what seemed like an eternity, Nick had laid beside me listening to me tell the story of that tattoo that I had never told anyone else.

\*\*\*

It started shortly after my mom found me on the bathroom floor of her clinic, bleeding and covered in vomit. Although my mother had not judged me for my choices that led to my predicament, she did scold me for going to the extreme measures that I had gone to.

"You could have killed yourself, Charlotte. What would I have done if I lost you?" she asked as she sat beside my bed a few days later. I still didn't quite feel like myself and my bed was the only place that felt safe, secure, and welcoming.

"I'm sorry," I said. The tears had started to gather in the corner of my eyes.

"Things happen, Charlotte. Sometimes it feels like we are alone, but you don't have to give in to those feelings. I will always be there to help."

I nodded. I believed her, but it still didn't dampen the feelings of guilt. In fact, it only made it worse because I continued to feel as if I had let her down. This guilt led to feelings of anxiousness and uncertainty, which began to escalate when I went back to school.

No one knew about what had happened. The secret was safe between me, Jia, and my mom, but that didn't stop the paranoia. Sometimes in the lunch line I would hear girls snickering behind me who would turn the other way when I looked at them. I always assumed they were talking about me, even though I knew it was impossible that they knew. If they were laughing it was because I had toilet paper on my shoe or my hair was parted oddly. But that didn't stop the irrational thinking. That is what the therapist called it, "irrational thinking," which made it sound like a condition all of its own accord.

I felt like I was constantly walking around town with a cartoon bubble over my head that said, "Yep, I'm one of those girls; used and dirty." When these thoughts would take over, the only relief was incessant scratching. Up and down, up and down, thirty or forty times until there were red welts on my flesh. For a while, this worked. It calmed me. But then it stopped working.

When I left for college, I thought that I had put the past behind me. I hadn't seen or spoken to Bobby since the accident. I had taken care of the one thing that connected us and I wanted nothing more than to forget every single moment of that part of my life. But I couldn't. The nightmares started when I was away and I felt incredibly homesick. I had wanted to get out of that suffocating farm community so bad, but once I made it to a city of millions I still felt stuck, exposed, and unable to hide.

At first the feelings only happened once a week, sometimes once every two weeks. When guilt started to strangle me I cut it off, literally. All it took was a pair of manicure scissors, tweezers, or even a nail file to saw away the culpability. Drawing blood didn't scare me. It should of, but I was numb and it felt good. But as most wicked actions do, things escalated quickly. I went from piercing, jabbing, and cutting at my body once a week to making it a daily ritual.

I always had something at my disposal to make the job easier. My purse was filled with enough pens to get the job done if I couldn't wait until I got back to my dorm room. One night my roommate confronted me. Her name was Tasha and she was from upstate New York, where the leaves always turned brilliant shades of red, orange, and yellow in the fall; snow blanketed the ground just in time for Christmas, and the maple syrup was homemade. In a word, she came from perfection. She must have found my insanity alarming or amusing. At that point in my life I wasn't sure I was able to tell the difference.

"Charlotte, is everything alright?" she asked.

I was sprawled out on my twin-sized bed listening to Nirvana and pretending to study as I read the same sentence over and over.

My arm was throbbing and on fire from my latest assault. "Peachy," I said. Tasha was a tolerable roommate, but I didn't want her to get the wrong idea that we'd be friends and sorority sisters for life, so I kept her at arm's length. Truth be told, I kept most people at arm's length.

"Are you sure?" she pressed.

"Positive." My positivity didn't persuade her. She stayed standing at the foot of my bed, her hands in her back pockets, biting her lower lip.

"Well, it's just you left some bloody tissues in our bathroom."

"I cut myself shaving. Sorry. I'll pick them up."

"This isn't the first time."

I sighed. "Okay, Tasha, bad roommate etiquette. I get it. Won't happen again."

Tasha pressed on. "I've noticed that your arm has been looking pretty bad."

"How's that?" I asked, instinctively pulling at my sleeve.

"Well, we *are* roommates and sometimes when I come back and you are resting or sleeping in I can see it. Plus, you wear long-sleeves all the time and, like I said, there are a lot of bloody tissues in the bathroom."

"You got it all wrong," I insisted. "Besides, I thought you were an economic science major, not a psychology geek."

"Charlotte, I don't want you to hurt yourself. Do you need to talk to someone?"

"I'm fine. You don't have to lose sleep over me."

Looking back at that time of my life I hated the person I had become. This person, she appeared so quickly, too. I hardly ever looked in the mirror anymore because I was afraid of who might be staring back at me. I was sure I wouldn't recognize her.

It wasn't more than 48 hours after I had that conversation with Tasha that I got a knock on my dorm room door. I opened it and found my mother standing on the other side. She was agitated. All the signs were there; the hair that was more out of control than usual, her jacket was ruffled, and I even think she had on two different shoes.

"Mom? Is everything okay?" I asked.

She didn't answer me. Instead, she dropped her suitcase, grabbed my left arm, and pushed up my sleeve. I winced. The fibers of my sweater scraped away newly formed scabs as my mother inspected the injuries. "What is this?" she asked. "What is this, Charlotte?"

I looked over at Tasha, who was slowly taking her headphones off her ears. She refused to meet my gaze. "I'll be back later," she said as she scurried out the door.

I backed into the room, pushing my sleeve down. My mom tried phrasing the question a different way. "Why are you doing this to yourself?"

How could I answer that question when even I didn't know? "It's not a big deal."

"Yes, Charlotte! Yes, it is a big deal. When I get a phone call from some young lady I don't know telling me that she is afraid for you, that is what I consider a big deal."

"How'd she even get your number?"

"How? What?" Mom threw up her hands, exhausted with my lack of concern for my own well-being. "Who cares how she got my number? Do you think I asked? No, I drove straight through the night to get to the bottom of why you are doing this to yourself."

She was angry, but I could also see she was frightened. My mom was one of those people who was always in control. Very little rattled her. "It's an occupational hazard," she had told me once. "I can't let fear, uncertainty, or any other pointless feeling rattle me when I am delivering a baby or even conducting a breast exam. Patients always feed off of your reactions, which is why I have to be as impassive as possible until the very last second." She wasn't controlling her emotions as she stood in my dorm room demanding answers.

My explanation for why I had resorted to self-harm, which was "I don't know," was not acceptable to my mother. The first order of business was to get me onto a psychiatrist's couch as soon as possible. As soon as the offices opened at nine am, my mom was making phone calls, while I lay on the bed curled in a fetal position. I was humiliated, but mostly scared. Next, my mom gathered everything she could find in my room that I could possibly use to inflict damage onto myself.

"This isn't necessary," I protested.

"Of course it is. It is absolutely necessary, Charlotte Laurel Day. I am not going to lose my daughter." Now that I know the things I know I wonder if she had been thinking about the baby girl she had given up.

"I can just go buy more," I admitted. "Besides, you don't need instruments to hurt yourself."

My mother's face fell, then her cheeks flushed red with anger. She instructed me to sit down on the bed. "Give me your hands." She dug the manicure scissors out of the trash bag and one by one cut my nails. "Whatever it takes, Charlotte. Whatever it takes because I love you and I will not let you destroy yourself over one mistake."

I was tempted to say, "Yes, but what about two, three, or four mistakes?" Instead, I kept quiet and watched my nails get clipped and sawed down into nubs.

## Chapter 19 – Harold
*Present Day*

"Did you know my father?" Charlotte asked.

Harold sighed. More questions. That is all this girl ever did was ask question after question after question. She was like a toddler in a woman's body. The only reprieve he had from her incessant hounding about this and that was when they had stopped at a hotel in Lake City, Florida because she was too tired to drive and refused to let him get behind the wheel.

In all of his years that his feet touched the soil, this was the first time he had ever stepped foot in a hotel. Even when he and Isabel were married they stayed home, honeymooning in the familiarity and security of their home. While others may have been taking off to exotic locations, they were perfectly content in their marital bed counting each other's freckles and making plans for the future. Harold wasn't quite sure how to act when they arrived at the establishment appropriately named The Sleep Inn. The front desk clerk was not particularly friendly, but then again it was two o'clock in the morning.

"We don't take cash," the clerk informed Harold when he

tried to pay for his room with a Ben Franklin and an Abraham Lincoln that he was none too happy to part with. It seemed like a lot of money to pay when you were only staying for a few hours.

"What do you mean you don't take cash? Who doesn't take cash?" Harold argued.

"You have to have a credit card to reserve the room, sir. You know. For incidentals."

"Incidentals? What does that mean?"

"Like if you trash the room."

Harold narrowed his eyes. "Do I look like I am going to trash a room?"

The clerk smirked. "We get all kinds here."

"I left my credit cards at home. I never travel with them." Harold felt humiliated. He noticed Charlotte pretending not to eavesdrop by the attraction brochures display, but it was quite obvious she was listening.

"Yeah, that makes sense," the clerk said. "Because traveling with cash is so much safer."

"Oh, for the love of God and everything holy," Charlotte exclaimed. "Can you be any more disrespectful? This gentleman does not need to be goaded and made fun of by a kid who still uses zit cream. Put his room on my card and give him a key."

With his key in hand, Harold thanked Charlotte. She waved him off. "No thanks needed. Let's just get some rest."

It took him a few minutes to figure out how the key, which was actually a card, worked, but when he finally got the door open he collapsed on the bed and fell into a deep, peaceful sleep.

***

The next morning, Harold and Charlotte sat at a table in the café next to the hotel, grabbing a quick breakfast before they got back on the road.

"So, did you know my Dad?" Charlotte asked again.

"Everyone knew your father."

155

"What was he like?" she asked.

"We weren't friends." Harold said.

"But I thought you liked him?"

"That doesn't mean we were friendly." Harold knew he should bite his tongue and let the questioning die. The least responsive he was the better for everyone, but he was tired. Too many years had passed. He had too many regrets. He was alone and he was just so damn tired of trying to live in the shadows of lies. Even he was surprised when the words tumbled from his lips. "I wasn't friendly with your father. I was jealous of him."

***

When Martin Day rolled into town in the spring of 1971 he created quite the frenzy. When this random man first showed up, strolling along Main Street, the gossipy hens and roosters created their own stories. Even the men in town were up in arms about this stranger encroaching on their territory. As is par for the course in small town America the stories became more and more outlandish as they were told and passed along from one person to the next.

"I hear he's an actor from Hollywood here to scout a location for a new movie," Mabel said while she and Isabel were working on stuffing envelopes for the church's annual fundraiser.

Isabel dismissed her and winked at Harold who had retired to the backyard lie in his hammock and finish a crossword puzzle he had started two weeks ago. "He's not nearly handsome enough to be a movie star. Perhaps he's on the run from the law and hiding out here like Jesse James."

"Margaret mentioned that she saw him at the bank depositing a large amount of cash. Which makes it appear that he plans to stay put for some time."

"Why don't you ladies just ask the gentlemen what his plans are?" Harold interrupted.

Mabel rolled her eyes. "Harold, that would be just plain rude."

"Yes, rude," he agreed. "Because talking behind his back is better manners."

It didn't take Harold long to find out what Martin Day was up to when the man showed up in his office a few days later. He strolled into Harold's office wearing a tweed sports coat with patches on the elbows, tan slacks, and a button down shirt. The only time the men in this town dressed that nicely was for a funeral or on Sunday. Everyone in town was still counted for and as far as Harold knew, it was still several days until Sunday. Martin held out his hand and introduced himself.

"No need for that," Harold said. "Everyone already knows who you are. You've created quite a stir."

Martin laughed. "I suspected as much."

"You have plans to stay long?"

"As long as everyone will tolerate me," Martin said. When he smiled his teeth were as white as alabaster. You didn't see many teeth like that in a place where nearly three-fourths of the population either chewed or smoked a couple packs a day. "I'm actually here about some property."

"Really? Which property?" Harold was used to handling all sorts of legal affairs from divorces to traffic court to real estate transactions. He was what one would call a "diversified legal professional."

"It's off Butler Road about five miles outside of town. About 250 acres, I reckon. Was told that it can support corn, soy beans."

"You planning on farming?" Harold asked.

"Maybe, maybe not. I haven't made up my mind. I'm a mechanic by trade. Born and bred in the Kansas City area. Was passing through here on my way to bigger and better things when I saw a for sale sign on that property and realized you don't get bigger and better than that."

"That's a lot of land for one man to tend to," Harold had said.

"Plan on moving my mom and dad out here, too. Maybe it will be a family adventure. We could build a couple of houses, a few miles apart, mind you, because a young bachelor like myself needs his privacy, and we'll see what transpires. I'm surprised that the land is still available quite frankly," Martin said. "I'd have thought one of the other families would have purchased it by now."

Harold perched on the edge of the desk, crossing his arms in front of him. "The reason it hasn't sold is Sylvie Gold."

"That's a pretty name," Martin said.

"Don't let the name fool you. She's as tough as they come around here and has refused to sell the property to anyone."

"She owns it?"

"Not all of it. She owns a small sliver that belonged to her parents years and years ago." Harold hesitated for only a brief second before continuing. "When her father was killed nearly twenty years ago she disappeared and the property was left in limbo. That one sliver was annexed into the adjacent property by the current owners, but it wasn't done legally. It's a complicated matter, but basically it means that without all the owners' approval the deed can't be transferred. The land can't be sold."

"Why doesn't she just purchase it all?" Martin asked.

"Like I said. It's a lot of land. Besides, I think Sylvie, I mean Dr. Gold, likes to have control over it."

Martin pondered that. "I'll talk to her and see what kind of compromise we can't work out," he said.

Harold laughed and shook his head. "You are a brave fella."

The compromise was marriage. It seemed to happen so quickly that it was hard to believe. Harold had never imagined that Sylvie would ever marry. He didn't know why he felt this way. Maybe it was his wounded ego and pride that, after all these years, still refused to be forgotten. More than likely it was plain and simple jealousy.

He wasn't exactly sure why he was so envious of Martin. Harold loved and adored Isabel more than anyone and she made him feel whole. But that didn't stop feelings of resentfulness from festering underneath his skin when he witnessed Sylvie and Martin walking in town together or when he emerged from the apartment near her practice early in the mornings, wearing the same clothes from the night before. He figured that as long as Sylvie stayed unattached, she would still be somewhat his. He knew that was irrational thinking, but it permeated his thoughts nonetheless.

"What crawled up your britches and died in your underpants?" Mabel asked Harold one morning when she and he were on their way to the senior center to visit their father.

After Harold and Isabel's wedding, their mother had begun complaining of indigestion on a daily basis. Once Mabel finally insisted that their mother be seen by a doctor, they discovered that she had a tumor the size of an orange forming in her upper stomach. It was cancer and it took her swiftly. Since passing away, Harold's father had seemed to steadily decline. Dementia overtook his cognitive abilities and made it impossible for him to live alone. Isabel had demanded that they open their home to him and she tried to care for him, but his constant wandering from the home worried both of them. The railroad tracks still ran through town and hosted a daily train. Harold and Isabel were afraid that one day he would wander off and unintentionally catch the train in the most unpleasant of ways. Eventually they decided to send him to Golden Oaks Senior Center.

"Nothing," Harold insisted. "Some of us don't need to talk incessantly."

Mabel prodded a bit more. "Sylvie and Marty are getting married next week. Could that be what's bothering you?

"Why should I care?"

"Thought maybe you were still holding a torch for her,"Mabel said.

"Not likely," he responded. "I have my own wife."

"And she's much too lovely for an insensitive lug like you."

"I know," he agreed thinking this would shut her up. The senior center was still another ten minutes away.

"They aren't having a huge ceremony. I'll be standing in as maid of honor, of course."

"Of course," Harold murmured.

"You're not planning on showing up at that wedding making

a fool of yourself are you?" Mabel asked.

"I wasn't invited," he reminded her.

"Just the same. Stay home and forever hold your peace, brother."

***

Shortly after the wedding, Sylvie and Marty began building the farmhouse. It took nearly six months to build, because a brutal winter set in, delaying construction. But nearly a year after Martin Day had shown up in town, the home was completed and Harold lost track of Sylvie. He no longer saw her as often. Sure she showed up at her practice every day, but when the appointments were over and the patients went home she locked up the front doors and took off in a direction farther and farther away from Harold.

Ever since that one conversation they had in Millie's when Sylvie had surprised him with her return, they hadn't properly spoken. It was as if they were practically strangers. And then one day she turned up pregnant. Even though she and Marty had been married for quite some time it still seemed sudden. Harold assumed that since Sylvie and Marty were well into their late thirties that they had no intentions of starting a family. But seeing Sylvie with her swollen belly proved Harold wrong and severed whatever ties to the past were between him and her.

Once the baby was born, it was even stranger to see Sylvie with a child. "She's such a doting mother," Isabel noted after spying mother and child in Schultz's Market.

Harold dismissed his wife's remarks. He was perfectly content holding tight to his feelings of animosity even if there was no reason for it. "It's easy to be doting to an infant. They haven't tested your patience. All they do is eat, sleep, and shit their pants."

Isabel placed her hands on her hips and gave him her serious stare. "I sincerely do not know how you can find anything unpleasant about a baby. Really, Harold. If you aren't careful you are going to turn into a grumpy old man long before your time and then I will have to leave you to find myself a more jovial old man to spend my time with."

Harold knew she was joking, but nonetheless he knew he had to keep his feelings of resentfulness away from their marriage. While he didn't think Isabel would be upset that he and Sylvie had a summer romance (could you even call it that?) all those years ago, she would be disturbed to learn that he wasn't able to let it go. But he *wanted* to let it go. He loved his wife more than his own life and didn't want to do anything to hurt her. So slowly, Harold began to think less and less of Sylvie and he turned his focus on starting his own family. If he had known then that it would be pointless, would he have tried? Harold couldn't answer that question.

\*\*\*

About six years after Sylvie and Marty got married and built their home on that secluded land outside of town, trouble started brewing. Harold smelled a faint whiff of this trouble when he stopped by Millie's after work one evening. Isabel had her book club friends over again and she wanted the house to herself. Most women in town had to fight tooth and nail to keep their husbands off the bar stools, but on those nights when a new book had to be picked apart and discussed, Isabel couldn't wait to get rid of him.

Harold didn't care much for the noise and the rowdy nature of the scene at Millie's. He wouldn't admit it to anyone, but he missed those days when root beer floats were the strongest drinks served. "Make it a double, that's two scoops, Howie," his dad would say when Harold would go into town with him. That was so long ago, yet the memories were still quite vivid. Unfortunately, both the root beer floats and his dad (or at least his memories) were gone and all Harold had left was a tall draft filled to the top with a grown man's bitter brew.

"What says you, Harry?" Bart Cullins asked, plopping down on the barstool next to Harold and rudely taking a sip of his draft. He grimaced when he swallowed. "Shit, Harry. That stuff tastes like watered down piss. You need something that will light a fire in your nether regions and make your old lady beg for more."

Harold hated Bart Cullins. He loathed him. He despised him. He could barely reconcile the fact that this man was an actual human. The hateful, disrespectful words that vomited from his mouth made Harold cringe and yet he continued to interact with the man for reasons that he would never understand. This would be one of his biggest regrets.

"I've got me a legal problem, Harold. Do you think you can help me legal problem?" Bart asked. Harold was pretty certain he had been drinking since the middle of the afternoon. His words were thick and his eyes were ugly with bourbon. Bourbon never made anyone's eyes pretty. He remembered the permanently fixed stare that Sylvie's dad had. Of course, it was hard to forget when his face had been so close to his that night when everything went wrong.

"Depends on the problem."

"You see, I think my wife is fixed on screwing me over."

Harold took a swig from his beer. The faster he finished it the faster he could beg off. "Sounds like a marital problem, Bart. You should consult with a priest."

"She's got a thing for that Marty Day fella. You know, Sylvie's husband? "

"I know who Martin Day is. But I don't think you have to worry. Why would she have an affair with him when she's got a winner like you," Harold said his voice teetering between sarcasm and wit.

Bart regarded him for a moment, trying to figure out if he was being made the butt of a joke, but the copious amounts of alcohol in his blood stream fueled his ego. "I wonder that myself, but some women, they just can't keep their legs together. You get what I'm saying?"

"I think you need to go home and sober up. Take a walk and get some fresh air. Addie wouldn't do anything to hurt you." What Harold really wanted to say was that Addie wouldn't do anything to piss Bart off because she, like most of everyone else in the town, was scared of him.

"Don't be so quick to defend that little slut. I saw her talking to him and Sylvie during the Cornfest just last week. Ever since their little chit-chat session she's been humming and praising the Lord with this song and that song. Only a woman getting it from someone other than her husband could be that happy."

"Like I said, Bart, go take a walk until common sense returns. And tell your wife I said hello."

The situation between Bart and Marty Day escalated as the weeks passed. Bart couldn't stay sober long enough to keep common sense between his ears. He showed up frequently at the auto repair shop Marty had opened in town, insinuating this and that, giving anyone within earshot quite a show. Isabel had been in Marty's shop one morning, inquiring about new tires for the Oldsmobile that had belonged to her father and was on its last leg. Tires were the least of that car's concerns.

"It was horrible," she told Harold. "The way that man got in Marty's face, poking him in the chest with his dirty fingers, and spittle flying from his mouth. Such an unnecessary scene."

Because curiosity got the better of him and because Isabel liked it when Harold attempted to participate in a conversation, he asked, "What did Day do?"

"He just took it. He didn't raise his voice or walk away. He let Bart wail and howl like a toddler throwing a tantrum. My Lord, it took everything in my power not to go in there and give him in the sweet spot."

Harold smiled. He loved it when Isabel got herself in a tizzy. "I would have paid a year's salary to see that."

"No, Harold, that would have been worth at least two year's pay."

"Day needs to deck him. Bart won't stop until someone puts him in his place. But no one's ever done that. They don't have the guts."

Isabel shook her head. "I disagree. Marty wasn't scared of

him. He seemed to pity him."

"Well, then that is a shame because from where I stand Martin Day should be very afraid of Bart Cullins."

## Chapter 20 – Charlotte
*Present Day*

"Do you know how your father died, Charlotte?" Harold asked after recounting his tale.

We had stopped at one of those infamous Florida rest stops that sat in the middle of the highway and resembled a small shopping mall than an actual rest stop. Harold had needed to stretch his legs and use the bathroom for the fifth time in what seemed like as many hours. His bladder was worse than mine and I was the pregnant one. We were sitting in the congested food court nursing sodas, weary from traveling and storytelling.

I had been the one to open the can of worms because I wanted answers, but now I wasn't sure that I wanted to learn the true circumstances surrounding my father's death while a couple of bikers gobbled down Whoppers at the table next to me. But since there really isn't ever a good way to receive this sort of information, I figured this might be the only chance I got to finally learn the truth.

"My mom didn't like to talk about it," I said.

Harold took a sip from his straw and nodded in acknowledgement. "Can't say I'm surprised. Some people prefer to keep their sadness hidden and locked deep inside. You know when your father passed your mother didn't step into town for two whole months. She stayed in that farmhouse with you and her grief. Isabel actually stepped in for a while at your mom's office performing midwifery tasks for the easy pregnancies and referring the high risk ones to other doctors a couple towns away."

This surprised me. I couldn't recall my mother ever missing a baby's birth or not attending to her patients. But lately, lots of facts about my mother surprised me. It is funny how death can give birth to a new life; paint a different portrait, so to speak.

"She never mentioned me in regards to your father's death?" Harold asked.

"Why would she?"

"Are you sure you want to know these stories?"

"They are a part of who I am," I said.

"You sound like my Isabel." Harold looked away from me.

"Do you miss her?" I asked.

"That's not what this story is about."

"Okay. Then tell me about my father."

"It wasn't an accident. It was murder, plain and simple, disguised as an accident." Harold said.

My breath caught in my chest. Murder was primal. It changed the tone of death in an instant, chipping away at the peacefulness of passing. Tainting the soul and leaving a smudge mark on the person's legacy. It frightened me. I wasn't sure I wanted Harold to continue. I wasn't sure I could handle the grisly details because I knew if I asked he would give them to me. I also wasn't entirely sure why I was assailed by such powerful emotions. I didn't really remember the man. The love I felt for him was love radiated from my mother. Her love for my father was something that she passed onto me as easily as eye color or hair color. It was an inherent trait, something I was given no control over.

"Go on," I said.

"Well, your father had the bad luck of being on the receiving end of Bart Cullins' jealousy."

"Cullins? As in Bobby Cullins' father?" I asked.

Harold ignored my question. "He thought that his wife was having . . . er . . . relations with your father."

"Was he?"

"Not at all. Everyone knew that Martin loved your mom. He was just one of those men who had a leading man's good looks and could capture a woman's heart with a smile without ever intending to. The problem was that Marty didn't know how that could work against him when there was a jealous husband thrown into the mix. He was naïve."

Harold wiped his brow with a flimsy napkin that had been left on the table by the previous customers. "Bart got in Martin's face several times, confronting him at the shop a couple of times. I just don't think your father took Bart's threats seriously. It wasn't hard to do. That man was typically several sheets to the wind at any given hour and one could dismiss his rants as nothing but drunken soliloquies. Even so, most people knew better than to go to bed without keeping one eye open when Bart was gunning for them. "

"So, he was gunning for my dad," I repeated.

"There's no doubt about that."

"What happened?"

"After several weeks of Bart verbally assaulting your father he decided to put a plan into motion. He enlisted his wife's help, against her will I might add. A lot of people looked down on Addie Cullins before and after your father's murder, but if one's being honest with themselves they might want to ask themselves what they would have done in her situation."

"I don't understand." I said this, but things were actually becoming clearer and clearer.

"Bart's abuse wasn't quiet. It was blatant and brutal."

"Why didn't anyone stop it?" I asked. When I was in college there were women's groups all over campus that helped women who were in abusive relationships. Safe homes were available for women and their children all over the city. Turning the other cheek these days wasn't an option. If you knew someone needed help, you gave them help.

"Small towns, Charlotte, are good for two things; gossip and denial. No one wanted to get messed up in their domestic situation. Things were different back then."

I contemplated his explanation or dismissal; I wasn't entirely sure how to categorize his response. I supposed it didn't matter because it wouldn't change anything now, but this information certainly put some things in perspective for me and made me realize why Bobby was the way he was. While he may not have turned out to be an abusive husband like his father, he saw enough violence and dysfunction to form tendencies that scared my mom. I guess it was true that mothers know what's best for their children. I felt tears building behind my eyes as I wished I hadn't realized this so late.

"Anyway," Harold continued. "He had Addie call Marty at the shop the morning of the accident. Bart told her to tell Marty that the tires were squawking and that she was afraid to drive into town because the problem seemed to get worse at high speeds. Would he come out to their place to take a look at it? So Marty shows up and takes the car for test drive to see what he hears." Harold stopped. "You know it's not a happy ending, Charlotte."

I blinked and that's when I felt the wetness on my lashes. Harold became a blur in a tan suit. "I know. But how do you know all of this?" I asked.

Harold gripped the edges of the table and looked down at his lap. His body began to shake and for a brief moment I was afraid that I had pushed him too far. That he was having a heart attack or a stroke, but then I realized that the convulsions were caused by a deep inconsolable sobbing. When he looked up at me our tearful eyes locked and he confessed, "Because I defended him."

## Chapter 21 – Harold
### *1976*

Stupidity, arrogance, fear, jealousy, and even excitement to be part of a murder case drove Harold to stand by Bart's side when the accident investigation turned up indisputable evidence that the brakes had been tampered with on the Cullins' car. The car that Martin Day was driving on the morning he died. Was he proud that he succumbed to Bart's will once more? That was a preposterous question, but one that Isabel asked nonetheless.

"Proud? No, I'm not proud. But they always taught me in law school that everyone deserves the right to a fair trial," I argued.

Isabel didn't buy it. "That is bullshit, Harold! You don't even like practicing law. It was your fall back because you got injured." When she was furious with him she didn't mince her words.

Although this may have been true, he didn't appreciate her throwing his failures in his face when he was clearly making another bad decision. "I'm sorry I have disappointed you." It was all he could think of to say.

"Me? Look in the mirror. I think you'll find I'm not the only one you're disappointing."

At this point Harold hadn't had a chance to speak directly with Bart. It was Addie he had spoken to. She showed up on his doorstep out of sorts and talking so fast that she stumbled over her words, stuttering something unbelievable. The only words that he could catch were "dead" and "Sylvie." He remembered how his heart had quickened, threatening to burst from his chest. As usual, Isabel, calm and collected under pressure, came to his side and led Addie into their home. This is when she related the events of the morning.

"Were you having an affair?" Harold had asked.

Addie gave him a disgusted look. "Why is a woman always the cause of a man's problems? No, I wasn't having an affair with Martin. I barely talked to him. The affair was one of Bart's deranged, paranoid illusions."

Harold had felt slightly disappointed that he had been right that nothing was going on. He wanted a reason to dislike Martin. He wanted to feel entitled to his jealousy and resentment, but instead he only felt guilty that he had wanted Marty to be vermin like him. Of course Marty wasn't vermin. Sylvie would never accept that type of relationship. Isn't that why she had rejected him so easily?

"I'm not sure what I can do for you, Addie." Harold had stated.

"Keep him out of jail," Addie demanded.

Isabel, who had been quiet up to that point, had frowned at Harold and then addressed Addie. "With Bart behind bars you'll be safe."

Addie had rolled her eyes. "How will I support myself? You know I married that man when I was basically a child myself. There is no way that I can find a job to support myself and my children. Without Bart's income how will I survive?"

"How will you survive when he comes home?" Isabel had asked.

"That isn't any of your concern." Addie said. "Besides, with Marty gone Bart will calm down. We'll manage."

Bart's trial lasted a mere three days and was a farce from the very beginning. Harold knew that the only reason charges were filed against him was because the county prosecutor was under the gun to get a few more convictions on his resume before he applied for a judgeship. But even the prosecutor knew that it was a waste of everyone's time. Although there was definitive proof that the car's brakes were tinkered with, Harold knew that without Addie's testimony there would be no way to prove that Bart had intentionally done it. In fact, as Harold argued when it was his turn to cross-examine the deputy in charge of the crash investigation, anyone could have messed with those brakes.

"Deputy Fletcher, you said that you believe that someone intentionally tampered with the brakes on Bart and Addie Cullins' 1968 Oldsmobile Cutlass. Is that your testimony?" Harold had asked.

"That is correct."

"You also stated that you came to this conclusion because there was no brake fluid spilled at the accident scene. Is this correct?"

"Again, that is correct."

"Is it possible that this was undetectable due to the nature of the accident?"

"Not in my opinion, no, sir. The accident was a one-car accident and the wreckage was limited to the vehicle Mr. Day was driving. Due to the force of the collision when Mr. Day's car, excuse me, the Cullins' car, hit the side rail of the bridge and plunged in the creek bed below, there should have been a noticeable amount of brake fluid leaking from the vehicle, but it was not detectable."

"Could the fluid have flowed into the creek water, therefore making it undetectable?"

"No, sir, "the Deputy insisted. "The vehicle never touched water. The creek bed was bone dry."

"I see," Harold had said. Changing directions he said, "Mr. Cullins wasn't a popular guy was he?"

"I'm not sure what you're getting at, sir."

"Over the course of many years on this job, I take it you responded to several incidents where Mr. Cullins was involved in altercations."

"The man in question, Mr. Cullins, made friends easily and, yes, he easily pissed them off. Generally, he was pissed with liquor when these incidents happened."

"Objection!" the prosecutor shouted. "Relevance, Your Honor. Intoxication is not a defense under the law. "

"Thank you for the primer, Mr. Prosecutor," the judge ruled. He looked at Harold. "Make your point, Klein."

"Would you say that there were people tired of being threatened and beaten to a bloody pulp by Mr. Cullins?"

"It's possible."

"You stated in your report that you believed the cause of the accident was a faulty brake system due to a drained reservoir. Is that correct?"

"That is correct."

"How do you know that Mr. Cullins tampered with the brakes?"

"The evidence."

"What evidence? Did Mr. Cullins confess this action to you?"

"Of course not. No, the evidence I am referring to is the drained reservoir and the absence of brake fluid when there should have been some at the crash scene. It's all in my report."

"Why would Mr. Cullins tamper with his own vehicle?"

"That is not information I am privy to, sir. Perhaps you should ask your client."

"With so many people tired of being browbeaten and on the receiving end of Mr. Cullins' fury, is it possible that someone else could have tampered with the brake fluid hoping to teach the defendant a lesson?"

"That's highly unlikely."

"But it's possible?"

Deputy Fletcher shifted in the witness stand. "I assume anything is possible."

"Were Mr. Cullins' fingerprints found on the brake line, the reservoir, or any other place near the brake system?"

"I can't answer that question."

"Why not?" Harold prodded. The courtroom went completely silent; even the court reporter's fingers paused in mid-air awaiting the answer. The only thing Harold could hear was the pounding of his heart in his ears. It sounded like a hammer. Boom-boom-boom, as it pounded one more nail into the coffin of the prosecutor's dying case.

"Because fingerprints were not dusted for."

"Isn't that odd?" Harold asked.

"Not in cases like this."

"Why is that?"

Tiny sweat pimples spoiled the young deputy's composure. He knew he was backed into a corner. "We don't dust for fingerprints in non-criminal cases."

"Non-criminal, you say. Then why are we even here?"

"The victim's wife asked for a copy of the accident report. She saw the notation about not finding any brake fluid and thought it suspicious, especially since she knew that the defendant had been unhappy with her husband and accusing him of illicit acts with his wife."

"Just so everyone in this courtroom is on the same page, let me get this straight. You arrested a man and charged him with murder for what you initially thought was a mere accident?"

"That is how it appears to be. Yes, sir."

"You have no fingerprints connecting my client with the faulty brakes?"

"No, sir."

"You have no statement from his wife or anyone else that Mr. Cullins intended to do harm to Martin Day on the morning in question?"

"No, sir."

"So, if I am to understand this correctly, you only arrested the defendant after his wife voiced her suspicions?"

"Yes, sir."

Harold chuckled as he turned to the jury. "Since when does the County Prosecutor make decisions based on a wife's grief? Perhaps we should be questioning *his* relationship with the deceased's wife."

"Objection!" the prosecutor yelled as he banged his fist on the table.

"Mr. Klein," the judge warned. "You are out of line. The jury will disregard those lewd and inconsequential statements from the defense."

Harold nodded, accepting the scolding. He knew there would be worse hell to pay when he stepped over the threshold into his home later that evening, because when he turned to walk back to the defense table he saw Isabel sitting in the back corner shaking her head.

"Do you believe Mr. Cullins' intentionally meant to harm Martin Day?"

"That is what the evidence says."

"But it doesn't really. Not if you take into account all the evidence – or lack thereof. Because the truth is there are a number of reasons why Martin Day was killed that morning and no one can ascertain beyond a reasonable doubt that the defendant was the cause of Martin Day's death. Is that correct?"

The deputy remained mute. The silence answered the question in its entirety.

Harold felt the adrenaline and excitement building in his chest. He had to do everything he could to contain the victorious smile that wanted to creep across his lips. Then, BOOM! The silence of the courtroom was shattered and any sense of victory that he felt dissipated, burning up like the fog by the morning sun because when he turned towards that sound he saw that the seat Sylvie had been occupying was empty. She had left the courtroom, but her venom lingered in the air.

## Chapter 22 – Charlotte
*Present Day*

Disillusionment isn't a bitter pill to swallow. No, it isn't that kind. Instead of going down in an uneven manner and leaving an after taste, it refuses to budge. It gets stuck in your throat and insists on gagging you until it is ready to put you out of your misery.

Here are the facts that I know about my mother. For the first eighteen years of her life she existed in that small rural community, scraping to get by and struggling to push past the public perception of her family until one day she walked away from it all without a word or an explanation. She had a baby by a man long before she ever met my father; a baby that she gave up. Somehow she put herself through medical school, which no one seemed to ever question or give a second thought to, including me. As if that was something that happened every day in the 1950s. She returned to that same community that had barely noticed her absence to secure a role that provided ample opportunity for every woman in the town to rely on her for support. Sweet revenge? She met my father, gave birth to me, lost her soul mate, and spent the subsequent years refusing to speak about the circumstances surrounding his death. During these years she filled her life as a fulltime parent and physician. She never complained. She never exhibited any signs of exhaustion at these equally grueling tasks. She simply seemed to exist like this on what now I realize may have been an auto-piloted response.

How, in 36 years, is this all I knew about my mother, I thought. Where did the blame lie? Could it have rested somewhere between the two of us? Clearly my mother had her secrets, but were these lies of omission meant to deceive me or were they natural lies? How well are children really supposed to know their parents?

Harold's stories had begun to fill in the blanks, helping me read between the years, but they weren't comforting. They were downright jarring. Scarier than any Halloween story I had ever been told because they were real. They painted my mother in a different color. When I thought of my mother I saw her in bright colors: gold, orange, bright green, and soothing purple. But Harold's stories splattered the canvas of my memories with black and red. It made me sad to discover that my mother had hidden her grief and her tendencies for payback from me, especially during those years in my life when I struggled with feelings of retribution for what Bobby had done to me and what I had ultimately done to myself.

"The morning that I came to your place to tell Sylvie about the accident at the Cullins', I walked away feeling like there was something she wasn't telling me. I couldn't have known what it was, but it stayed with me for a long time. It was only after Isabel got sick that I learned what your mother had done."

"What do you mean?" I asked.

"Isabel had felt a knot in her breast one morning. She had tried to get an appointment with her regular doctor at the clinic, but he was out on some fishing expedition and wasn't taking appointments for the next couple weeks. I suggested she go see Sylvie."

"She did," I said, remembering that day in Mom's office when we had argued over the joys of sex and the elderly.

"Yes, but only after I begged her to call for an appointment. You see, Isabel was ashamed. She may have forgiven me for representing that despicable man, but she hadn't forgiven herself for offering that forgiveness. She couldn't see how Sylvie could separate her from being my wife and her patient. Isabel already knew that the knot in her breast meant trouble, so when they met, Isabel asked her if she would be able to treat her without feeling hatred. That's when Sylvie told her that she had let vengeance and spitefulness make a decision for her that she had regretted and she wouldn't do it again."

"What did she do?"

"Isabel had been correct all those years ago. Addie Cullins had been to see Sylvie, but not at her office. At your farmhouse, the night before the accident or murder-suicide. That's what they call it nowadays, right? Anyway, she had driven out to your house that night and asked Sylvie for help securing an abortion. Sylvie turned her away. She wouldn't help her, but can you blame her? Why would she help the woman who had been part of the plan to kill her husband?"

I knew it was a rhetorical question, but I wouldn't have had an answer if one had been expected anyway. I let Harold continue talking.

"She told Isabel that she would never let those feelings interfere with a woman's life ever again." Tears had reemerged in Harold's voice.

Against my nature, I took his frail, limp hand into my own and searched his eyes. He looked at me with surprise. "It must have been hard to lose her."

"Six months," he said. "Six months to the day that she visited your mother she passed. The cancer was advanced and there wasn't much that anyone could have done to save her. I still miss her every single minute of every day. It's a pain that is sometimes too much to bear. But I am happy to feel it."

"Why?" I asked. Most people run away from pain. I couldn't imagine embracing it.

"Because it finally proved to me that I loved her more than your mother. I only wish I had realized this when she was alive so I could have stopped punishing myself for those feelings when the truth was Isabel was my world, my moon, and my stars. In death Isabel gave me peace."

I considered this sentiment and hoped that someday I would

find peace, too.

***

"Does it feel better knowing?" Nick asked.

"It feels complicated," I said, cradling the cell phone against my ear as I took off my shoes in the hotel room. After Harold confessed his role in the aftermath of my father's death, we drove another three hours to Boca Raton in total silence.

"It hurts my heart even more than kissing my mother's stone cold cheek," I admitted.

"Oh, Charlie. I wish I could be there with you. I should be there."

"Please, Nick. I love you, but being here wouldn't ease the hurt. I'm not even sure it's hurt. It might be more like guilt. I never realized how much pain my mom carried around with her. She put so much energy into taking care of me and putting up with all of my drama throughout the years."

"Maybe that helped her deal with what she couldn't control."

"Maybe," I said. "But it's not just guilt," I confessed.

"Then what?"

"Anger," I admitted. "I am just so angry at her, Nick. She's dead and do you know what that means? It means that she got away with it."

"Away with what?" he asked. I could hear the hesitation in his voice and knew he was contemplating how long he should entertain this conversation. I could see him now, pacing back and forth, running his hand through his hair, worry starting to play upon his brow.

"Without facing me and providing me with a proper explanation," I yelled.

"Charlie, you promised me you wouldn't get worked up."

"I'm fine, Nick," I said taking a deep breath and forcing myself to speak more calmly. "I'm not getting worked up. I am just trying to make sense of why she thought it was okay to not tell me she was dying. Why it was perfectly acceptable to keep a sister from me all my life. Why she decided that the best way to tell me about her was through a letter. It's a cowardly thing to do. I didn't realize my mother was such a fucking coward."

I collapsed on the bed, exhausted by my emotional outburst. I had bottled up my emotions for the past several days and I couldn't contain them any longer. They were like carbonated fizz, refusing to be confined by a bottle cap.

"People lie, Charlotte," he said. "They lie out of fear. They lie because they are afraid what another person will think of their actions, but mostly they lie because they want to protect the ones they love."

"Are we going to do that? Are we going to lie to this child about things, important things?"

Is that how it will be between this child and me? I never considered the possibilities of not sharing my life experiences with my child, but would it do him or her any good to know about every mistake I've made? Is the parent/child relationship an open book or is discretion the rule?

"We are going to tell this child that it is loved. As long as he or she is loved that is all they really need to know, right? And I am pretty sure that your mom loved you."

"She did," I admitted. "I always felt that love even when I wasn't the easiest person to love."

"So, there you go," Nick stated. "Let that knowledge of love carry you through these next days, weeks, months, and years."

I smiled at the cheesiness of his statements. "You sound like a preacher writing a Hallmark card."

"I can do singing cards," he said. I could hear the grin in his voice. "Would you like me to demonstrate?"

"No! Please keep those awful sounds to yourself."

Nick laughed and I smiled again. My heart was hurting a bit less and the world didn't seem quite so treacherous and deceitful. "It's going to work out the way it is meant to work out."

"It will," I said even if I was still a little bit doubtful. But Nick didn't have to know that. Like he said, all we needed to know is we were loved. So I told him I loved him, closed my eyes, and dreamed of nothing.

## Chapter 23 – Charlotte
*Present Day*

"Well," I said.

"Hmmm," Harold replied.

I grabbed the paper from his lap and studied the address. "Are you sure this is the right address?"

The neighborhood surrounded us from all sides. There were a number of vacant and abandoned buildings as well as two parking lots that advertised cheap, safe parking. At $15 per hour the rate was arguable and the safety factor was laughable. Graffiti embellished the sides of nearly every building within the vicinity, including the dumpsters and light poles.

"Maybe your electronic map is wrong," Harold offered.

"My GPS is not wrong," I argued.

"It seems defective. Or is it supposed to shout the same thing over and over again? Recalculating! Recalculating!"

"Stop it," I hissed. "That is not helping." I observed a couple of young men in hoodies and jeans, clothes way too warm for August in South Florida, walking towards one of the buildings at the end of the dead end street. There was a sign out front that looked like it was intentional writing, not street art.

"I'm nervous," Harold confessed. As I sat there observing the men and assessing the scene, he had begun to tap his foot against the floorboard, while smoothing the fabric of his pants. The steady beat of his foot and the swish of his hands against the fabric of his tan suit pants created an interesting sound that filled the silence. It was the beat of uncertainty and fear.

"Me, too, " I said. "I think the address we are looking for is over there." I pointed to the building the boys had walked into.

"Are you sure?"

I shrugged, took a deep breath, and widened my eyes. "I'm not sure of anything."

"Maybe we should go home," Harold suggested.

"We came so far," I said.

"So? What does that mean? Does it mean that we can't choose to say to hell with it?"

"For me it does. I'm here and I am going to see this through. I think you should, too." I crept the car closer to the building, giving Harold a little more time while I stalled a little myself.

The name of the building was the Hope House. That is what the sign said as I drove closer to the building. The address underneath the letters matched the address that Harold had given me, but it certainly was curious. I had expected to pull up to a traditional Boca Raton residence. The ones with the palms trees in the front and the stucco roofs with manicured yards and, yes, maybe even a flamingo or two if I was being stereotypical, but this was not what I expected. This building was nestled between a vacant lot with copious amounts of litter strewn about and another vacant building with some windows busted out. It reminded me of the hollowed-out buildings I had seen traveling along I-70 through St. Louis or in certain forgotten neighborhoods in Chicago.

I turned off the car and unbuckled. Harold just looked at me. "Are you coming with me?"

"In there?"

"Yes, in there. Enough stalling, let's just get this over with."

I held the door for Harold and handed him his cane. He seemed taken aback when I looped my arm through his to help him up onto the sidewalk. "I am not a damn invalid," he grumbled, but he didn't pull away. We both needed the other to hold us upright and make us put one foot in front of the other to get to the front door.

There were ten steps to that front door. It took about three minutes for us to climb the steps. Each step required patience and exertion. It was quite possibly the longest journey I had ever taken. When we reached the top step it felt like we had reached the summit of Mount Kilimanjaro. In fact, we both stopped and took in the moment, looking around and admiring our feat. We had climbed the ten steps, now all that was left was to ring the bell.

It wasn't quite a bell, but a buzzer. As we waited for the door to open we could hear heavy footsteps running back and forth inside. I saw the curtain that covered the front window flutter and I thought I caught a glimpse of an eye or maybe an ear, but then that small fragment of a face disappeared and the footsteps continued.

"Ring it again," Harold said.

This time I pushed hard and let my finger linger until I counted to five. "Holy Jesus and Mary," I heard a voice say. "Hold your knickers. I'm coming as fast as the Lord wills my feet to go."

When the door opened a slight, round African-American woman with her hair neatly cornrowed atop her head answered the door. She wore red glasses that reminded me of the kind that daytime talk show host used to wear. What was her name? Sally something. I couldn't remember. Mom hadn't been too keen on television and she referred to all daytime television as mind-numbing and exploitive. I was limited to Sesame Street for many, many years.

"Well," she huffed. "Ya'll aren't exactly what I was expecting. Thought Jorge ordered a pizza again when I specifically told him that he was cut-off. Last time he cost me $20 out of my own pocket because Lucy decided to raid the petty cash."

"Jorge?" I asked. "Lucy?"

The woman laughed, loud and with so much vigor that her double G bosom bounced up and down. She didn't seem to notice or care. "Never mind ya', girl. What can I do for you? Bringing donations from the church?"

"No, ma'am." Harold spoke up. "We are here to see Francis

McCabe."

The woman cocked her head and looked at him inquisitively. "Francis? Frannie? Oh, sweet Jesus! I haven't heard that name in years." She laughed hard again.

My heart sank. We came all this way for nothing. We were stupid. We should have called. Who shows up on a woman's doorstep after so many years and doesn't call? "So, she's not here?"

"Frannie?" the woman said. "Oh, Frannie's here. We just don't call her by her birth name. No, no. You are looking for Miss Hope. Come on in. Let's go find her."

The woman turned and started sing-songing down the hall toward the back of the building. "Frannie! Oh, Frannie. You got yourself some visitors."

I stood planted firmly in place unable to make my feet move. That's when I felt the jab of a cane in my calf. I glared at Harold. He glared back. "Go," he demanded.

We walked in the direction that the woman had gone. There was music coming from one room and I spied a young girl – Lucy? - sitting on a shabby couch reading a book and ignoring us. A younger boy, about twelve, peeked around the corner from another room and then ran off. This must have been the shadow face I saw in the window. We walked into the kitchen and I saw the two boys in the hoodies that I had seen when we pulled up. They were conversing in Spanish, laughing, and slathering Mayo on pieces of bread stuffed full of processed meat. My pregnant stomach heaved. One of the boys looked up and smiled, lifting his chin in acknowledgement. I raised my hand to return the acknowledgement and felt the cane in the back of my leg again. I ignored Harold, but made a mental note that we were going to discuss this cane business when we were alone.

Hushed whispers came from an office on the other side of the kitchen. When we reached the office, the door opened briskly and the woman who had spoken to us came out. "I'm sorry. Miss Hope is busy right now. You'll need to make an appointment."

"An appointment?" I asked like it was a term that I had never heard of before.

"Yes, an appointment. You know. You pick up a phone, dial our number, and schedule time to meet with Miss Hope."

I smiled, hoping that this woman and I could connect on a friendly basis. "It's not what you think. We really need to speak with her."

The woman looked me up and down then looked at Harold. She seemed remorseful and unhappy that she had been instructed to turn us away. "Not today. Like I said, she is busy."

I stood there quietly trying to figure out how to convince this woman that I needed to get past her when Harold startled us both. He smacked his cane against the hardwood floor and shouted, "No!"

Both the woman and I jumped. Harold banged his cane against the floor again. "No. That will not do. Move out of my way," he demanded.

The woman put both arms on her hips and stared Harold down. "Sir, if you think that you can make demands, you are out of your Alzheimer's mind." She patted her chest and continued, "I have me a knife, a cell phone, and a can of Mace in here. I am not afraid to use them on your ass."

Harold was undeterred. He used his cane like a blind man uses a walking stick, moving it back and forth, forcing the woman to dance a humorous jig to get out of the way. "Do what you must. But I am done having my future decided for me."

I pushed past the woman and followed Harold, thankful that I had been demoted from the leadership position. The door to the office was locked.

"I told ya'll she wasn't available to see anyone today."

Harold turned the knob several times, willing it to open and then resorted to banging on the door with all his might. This was not going the way I envisioned it. Did I think meeting this long lost daughter and sister would be a Lifetime movie moment with a melancholy soundtrack playing in the background and tears of laughter and joy? Yeah, I guess I did. Did I picture Harold going apeshit crazy, banging on an office door in an unfamiliar place that smelled like teenage musk and rotten garbage? No, this was not how I imagined this moment unfolding and yet this is exactly what was happening.

"Harold," I urged, reaching out to touch his shoulder. He shrugged me off and continued knocking. "Stop this! It isn't helping. Let's just go."

He stopped banging on the door long enough to stare me down. He enunciated his words very slowly so there would be no mistaking what he was saying. "I am not leaving. I am not leaving until this door is opened and I get to meet the woman that Sylvie took from me."

Harold raised his hand to start knocking again when I heard the lock click. I grabbed his arm and pulled him away. The door to the office opened and staring back at us was a ghost. The woman on the other side had strawberry blonde hair graying at the temples. Her gray eyes had specks of blue. Her aquiline nose and her small frame were the spitting image of my mother. The woman didn't seem surprised or angry to see Harold and I. Instead, she seemed defeated.

"I'm sorry, Miss Hope. I tried. I even threatened them with my arsenal." She thrust her chest out. This made the woman smile.

"It's okay, Janelle. Leave us, will you?"

"Are you sure? That one," she pointed to Harold, "seems a little too spunky for his Depends."

"Yes, please. Everything is perfectly fine." She then addressed us. She sighed and took her time before acknowledging us. "After all, we're family, right?"

# Part Four

*"If you cannot get rid of the family skeleton, you may as well make it dance."*

— George Bernard Shaw, *Immaturity*

## Chapter 24 – Francis "Hope" McCabe
### *Seven Months Earlier*

Hope hadn't needed to be told she was adopted. She didn't need a certificate with strangers' names typed on official paper with a notarized seal spelling out her parentage. The evidence of her birth was quite blatantly displayed every single second of her existence. To begin with there were the light colored eyes that no one on either side of her parents' ancestry shared. The coloring shared among her two older brothers, mother, and father was much darker; olive skin, eyes dark as coal nuggets, with dark hair to match. Hope was the glaring bright light that always illuminated family pictures and made passersby do a double take.

"It's from the Irish side, sweetie," her mother had told her with a tight smile when she was close to ten and a stranger on the street had joked about her being the white sheep of the family. Hope didn't buy the explanation. It was cheap and flimsy, especially since everyone knew Granddaddy O'Reilly had married her grandmother long after she had given birth to her father. Irish may have flowed through her veins, but she knew it didn't come from any man named O'Reilly.

There were other noticeable differences that weren't what one would consider genetic, but still played a role in Hope reaching the conclusion that their little family of five wasn't all-inclusive, at least in terms of blood and lineage. Family photos depicted pictures of Louis and Clive from as early as when they were in her mother's womb and then every three months after. Hope's pictures didn't start to appear on the fireplace mantel until around the first year mark.

"Where are my baby pictures?" Hope asked her mother the same day the stranger made the comment about her being the white sheep. She had begun giving her mother quite a deal of stress, asking rampant questions but receiving few answers.

Her mother was dusting the house to get it ready for a poker game her father was hosting that night. She gave an exasperated sigh and responded tersely, "Right there, Francis, on the mantel with your brothers'."

"Those are not baby pictures," Hope had informed her. "Those are pictures of a toddler. I want a baby picture."

"Oh, dear, please. There is so much to do before your father gets home. I'll get your baby pictures put on the mantel soon. Okay?"

Hope had nodded, secretly hoping her mother would follow through on her promise, but she knew better. Her baby pictures would never be displayed on the mantle like Louis' and Clive's because they didn't exist; maybe somewhere they existed, but not in boxes or photo albums in that house.

As Hope had grown and stretched into adulthood, she stopped wondering and started accepting. It was humorous the way her parents still insisted that she was their blessing, their surprise coming so many years after Clive was born. "Six years," her father boasted. "We waited six years for a little girl to come into our life and now you are a woman." He snapped his fingers. "That fast. It happened that fast."

Why they thought they couldn't tell her about her true biological parentage was baffling. Was she the daughter of a notorious mobster? Were her parents Peace Corps members forced to sacrifice their child so they could continue their mission only to die at the jaws of an angry crocodile on the Gandhis? Hope entertained these thoughts on nights when she was lonely and drank too much wine without enough friends. A lack of desire to put herself out in the world made her a prisoner to her kitchen table, spending too much time leafing through fashion magazines and imaging herself as the long-lost daughter of Princess Grace. When she got to this point in her musings she would dump the remnants of the wine, both in the glass and the bottle, into the sink and go to bed.

Did it really matter who her parents were? Not really. Not in the scheme of things because the life she was given by Ernest and Claudia O'Reilly was enough. She was loved, admired, and doted on. There wasn't anything in the world that those two people wouldn't do for her. They had bandaged her damaged knees countless times when she was learning to ride a bicycle without training wheels. They had stuck up for her when she had been called into the principal's office for pushing Mattie Owens off the jungle gym in the third grade, even though she had actually done it; they had believed in her innocence no matter what. They bought her clothes that were stylish even though they had disapproved and found the wide-legged bell bottoms utterly atrocious. As far as parents went she had no grounds or right to complain. This is why she stopped pressing for answers from a mother who refused to give them and a father who looked at her quizzically when she asked for stories about the day she was born. Perhaps this was because they couldn't imagine why she would think she belonged to someone else, when she so clearly belonged to them. Blood didn't make a family; sacrifice, memories, and a shared history made families. Blood was only biological matter.

So, she let it go. But like most matters in the past, even a past that hadn't been of her choosing, caught up to her. In the mid-1980s, her father became ill. It started out as nothing more than a case of bad heartburn that wouldn't quite go away. Five bottles of antacids and several specialist visits later he was diagnosed with Stage IV esophageal cancer.

"It's bad, Francis, really bad," he said one night as he lay in the hospital bed attached to IVs and other ominous monitors. The constant beeping of the monitors sometimes lulled Hope to sleep as she sat by her father's bedside, but most times they simply reminded her over and over that life was short and that the reverberations of a heartbeat only lasted for a few short seconds and then died.

As there always seemed to be, there were a few younger doctors who thought they could prolong his life, whether her father thought it was a good idea or not. Perhaps he would have preferred a treatment that would have ended it all right there, but at that point in his illness he was rarely lucid and unable to express his wishes. It seemed cruel not to let him go, but perhaps they all needed to hold on a little longer.

"A blood transfusion may prolong his life," a young doctor named Samuel McCabe had told Hope in the dim, dreary hallway of the cancer ward after a particularly bad day of excruciating pain and bouts of vomiting that produced nothing but vile smelling stomach acid.

"Is that really what is best?" Hope had asked. The doctor had beautiful eyes; they were green and sparkled when he smiled. Some may have called them feminine eyes, but Hope felt she could get lost in them and be perfectly content never finding her way home. Guilt radiated through her body for having these feelings, because for one her father was dying and two she already had a boyfriend, although he had found more and more reasons to avoid her lately. She couldn't blame him. Being around the constant smell of death could be overwhelming.

"It's a chance. Is it best? Well, that is debatable. Cancer is a hard disease on the family," he sympathized.

Hope shook her head. "It's harder on my father, you mean."

"Sometimes, but we can give him morphine to numb the pain. What can we give you?"

In order to go through with the blood transfusion all the family members had donated blood. To this day Hope couldn't say what it was about her blood that made the answer definitive that she had been born to a different mother and father. The technicalities were explained to her behind the closed doors of Dr. McCabe's office door, but she hadn't listened. He hadn't really had to tell her that she had been right all along, because what was she possibly going to do with this information? It wouldn't help her father survive. It wouldn't lessen her mother's grief. All it could do was create a rift that hadn't been there before. So Hope swallowed the truth, letting it go down her throat silky and smooth. And that is where it stayed buried for the next 28 years.

***

The months following her father's passing were easier than Hope had anticipated. While there were moments of sheer panic and morbid thoughts of mortality as well as deep, visceral sadness, there was a peacefulness that settled into her heart. It was as if her father's death had relieved her of the burden of knowing because it didn't matter anymore. Once this serenity filled her core, she began to reorganize her life.

First, she got rid of the boyfriend. He held no purpose in her life other than an average lover and a sub-par contributor to her happiness. Hope was tired of going through the motions of a relationship that didn't matter. When he was at work one day she packed up what little belongings there were of his at her house - he didn't even keep a toothbrush at her place; that should have always been a sign that the relationship was futile – stuffed them not so gingerly into a cardboard box and sat them on the curb outside of her apartment building. The act was liberating, watching him find the box, scratch his head, then walk away positively unaffected. It actually made her laugh. She should have been sad or insulted at his casual acceptance of their relationship ending, but she could have cared less. It was one more item to scratch off her to-do list.

The second decision she made was to pack up her own belongings and move north. She didn't have a clue what she would do. She had spent her twenties and early thirties working for various charities doing fundraising, clerical work, and a little lobbying now and then. Maybe if she moved north to a bigger metropolitan city like St. Louis or Chicago she could find a decent job that could marry those skills and provide her with a decent income. All she knew is that she had spent all her life being kissed and caressed by the South

Florida sun and she burned way too easily. It was time to move some place where it made logical sense to have hot chocolate in the winter and you could hunker down underneath a warm blanket while snowflakes made you a willing hostage in your own home. Besides, she had always felt drawn to the Midwest. It may just be a different shade of mundane, but that was fine with her.

It was a Thursday evening when the phone rang. She was wrapped up in folding laundry that had been sitting on the kitchen table for days and the shrillness of the ringer nearly made her pee her pants. Since the boyfriend (ex-boyfriend) had moved out it hardly rang. There weren't too many people in her life that needed her that urgently. They would just wait until they saw her.

"Francis O'Reilly?" a familiar voice inquired. She couldn't quite remember where she had heard the voice before.

She cradled the phone between her ear and shoulder, blowing a strand of untamed hair out of her face. "It's Hope," she said.

"Excuse me?"

"Nobody but my mother and father call me Francis. I prefer Hope," she had explained.

"Err, I see. Well, Hope, this is Dr. McCabe. From St. Luke's. Do you remember me? I was the physician assigned to your father, Ernest."

Hope put down the pair of granny pants she was folding. Dr. McCabe. She had certainly not forgotten the physician with the alluring eyes and the only other person who knew her secret. "Yes, I remember who you are."

"Oh, good," he exclaimed. She could hear the relief in his voice and could imagine the smile on his face. How is it that even months later she had been able to clearly remember the way the skin crinkled around his eyes when he smiled?

"Are you able to meet for coffee tomorrow? There is a restaurant across the street from the hospital. They serve horrible coffee, but I'll buy you a Danish that makes up for the bitter brew."

Hope had planned to pay a visit to her mother in the morning

193

to gently tell her about her plans to move away from Boca, but she figured she could go after meeting with Dr. McCabe. She couldn't imagine what he might possibly want. "That's an intriguing offer, especially since so many months have passed," she said.

He laughed and she felt as if she were weightless. *Snap out of it, Hope*, she told herself. *Get yourself together.* "It is. I wish I had more time to explain why I need to see you, but I just got called to go into surgery. Tomorrow at nine, okay?"

"Sure," Hope said. "See you then."

She hung up genuinely confused and pretty certain that her newly organized life was going to get rearranged all over again. She looked down at the granny pants she had sat on the table, contemplated their dullness and lack of appeal then picked them up and threw them in the trash. She was way too young to start acting like an old lady.

*** 

"Thank you for agreeing to meet with me," Dr. McCabe said when she sat down across from him at the restaurant.

He was wearing street clothes, his white coat and scrubs nowhere to be seen. If Hope had been remotely attracted to him during her father's illness, she was practically head over heels in love now as he sat across from her in a casual jeans and t-shirt. The muscles in his forearms flexed as he moved his hands. Dr. McCabe liked to talk with his hands. She wondered what else he could do with his hands. *Stop it*, she scolded herself. *You are acting like one of those women in a trashy romance novel. Get it together.*

"Well, you peaked my curiosity, Dr. McCabe. What could I do but meet you?"

"Run the other way as fast as you could?" he suggested, smiling. "By the way, it's Samuel. Or, Sam. Most people call me Sam."

"Sure," Hope said. "That's a nice name. So, what can I do for you?"

"A lot, I hope. You see, every year the hospital takes a local charity under its financial wing, so to speak, to help it flourish and thrive. Funds for private charities wax and wane depending on who's in office and what causes are deemed worthy enough for those funds."

"Or what causes will further a politician's career, you mean?"

"Absolutely! That is entirely the case most of the time, isn't it? Those that need help the most only get it if they are lucky enough to be desolate enough to make a difference in a rich, white guy's career. That is why the hospital tries to bridge the gap. This year the hospital has decided to work to create a safe haven for teens that have run away or are without a home for other reasons."

"That's admirable," Hope said, still not sure which direction the conversation was going in, but feeling foolish for thinking he had called her because he missed seeing her face once or twice a week during rounds and consultations. Nearly thirty-three years old and she was acting like an infatuated teen. The colder air up north would probably cure that.

"We, well, *I'm* not doing it for recognition. I get so tired of seeing these kids on the streets. They walk into the hospital on a daily basis, faking stomach pains or intentionally harming themselves just so they have a place to stay for the night. The streets are not kind to these children when the sun goes down."

"So what is your solution?" Hope asked.

"I'm hoping, no pun intended," he smiled at his silly joke, "that the solution is sitting in front of me. Your father told me that you are an angel. That you've spent the years since college helping those in need."

I waved him off. It was just like my father to talk me up as a saint when I was merely a sinner wearing decent and pretty clothes. "I hardly think that is true. My father liked to exaggerate. I did work for several non-profits, helping them with fundraising efforts, and writing a few grants here and there. But I would hardly call that angelic."

"Call it what you want, but I want someone like you."

"Like me?"

"Yes, I want someone young and talented to help me start a foundation. To help me make this year's charity case be more than that. I want you to help me make a difference in these young people's lives. Will you help me?"

It wasn't desperation in his voice that she heard. It was excitement and a true belief that she could be part of something big. This wasn't the plan. The plan was to start fresh somewhere far away from Boca where she could build a life that was her own. But when she looked into Sam's eyes she knew that plans were fickle and meant to be changed when the right opportunity came along. When she looked into Sam's eyes, she saw her future.

*** 

She and Sam had created a wonderful legacy together. Not just with the Hope House, which is what Sam insisted they call it one night during the initial planning stages, but together as a couple. It had only taken two more meetings to discuss plans for the Hope House before Sam had asked her out and only two months after that until they were racing to a 24-hour chapel in Palm Beach County to get married at two in the morning.

"That was rather fast," her mother had said in a tone that Hope couldn't decipher. "I thought there would be a wedding."

"There was," Hope had assured her as Sam stood by her side holding her hand and beaming from ear to ear even though he was already in hot water with his new mother-in-law.

Claudia O'Reilly crossed her arms in front of her and shook her head. "You know what I meant, Hope. Well, at least he's a doctor." Then her face softened and she walked toward Sam to embrace him. "A doctor who took wonderful care of your father and a man that I know will take wonderful care of you."

They were married for 22 years. Not long enough to be considered a lengthy marriage, but decidedly long by modern standards, when most marriages began to falter as soon as the vows were spoken. Since losing her father, Hope had lost her mother to an aneurysm and a niece to leukemia. She had witnessed several of the teens they had tried to help lose battles with addiction, depression, and other dangers that the big bad world offers, but none of these loses crippled her as much as losing Sam. Perhaps it was the sudden nature, the ripping away of his soul from hers without warning.

Sam loved to deep sea fish. He would spend hours on his small fishing vessel, the *Luna Sea*, dipping his pole into the blue waters of the Atlantic while the waves gently rocked the boat back and forth. He had tried to get Hope to go on these adventures with him, but even heavy doses of Dramamine couldn't keep the seasickness at bay. It was pointless. This was to be her husband's time for solitude.

"Please stay home," Hope had begged.

Sam was sitting at the end of the bed tugging his shoes on. The arthritis in his ankles made it painful to wear shoes that weren't boat shoes, but he refused to wear those until he was on the boat and safely out of the harbor. Hope could sense Sam was frustrated with her worrying. She did always worry when he was alone on the open sea in his boat, but she insisted that it was different this time. "Haven't you paid attention to the weather reports?"

"Yes, dear, you know I do. The storm is weakening off the coast. The forecasters don't expect it to be here until late this evening and it will be nothing more than a thunderstorm." He kissed her on the forehead and then kissed her again on the lips, lingering longer than usual, providing her with the opportunity to soak up his scent; ivory soap and mint toothpaste. "I will be home for dinner, hopefully with something tasty. Otherwise, I'll take you out for dinner."

There wasn't any way that Hope would have been able to convince Sam to stay off the *Luna Sea* that day, but he had been wrong. He wouldn't be home for dinner and the storm would gather strength once it ran into the warmer coastal waters. For three days, Hope had paced the length of the house waiting for news from the rescue crews and the Coast Guard. When two officers had shown up at her door instead of calling her on the phone, she fell to the floor, where she stayed for what seemed like an eternity.

The days and then months following Sam's death were a blur. Slowly, Hope lost sight of herself. She rarely entertained visitors. She lost contact with her brothers who had grown tired of reaching out to a ghost. Even the Hope House had seemed to mourn Sam. It fell into shambles as the neighborhood continued to implode. What had once been a safe haven for so many troubled and disadvantaged teens had turned into just another disappointment.

Near the one year anniversary of Sam's disappearance at sea – yes, there wasn't even a body that Hope could bury and visit – there was a knock on the door. Hope had been reluctant to answer it. She hadn't looked in a mirror in months, but was sure that her appearance was startling. Sam would be disappointed, but he had left her and she didn't care anymore.

She opened the door and Janelle stood on the other side. She worked at the Hope House as a sort of house mother; nurturing and providing for the youth like they were her own children. "They are my bonus children," she used to say. Hope and Sam had agreed with that sentiment since they emotionally adopted all the teens that walked through those doors, too.

"You like look shit, Miss Hope," Janelle blurted when the door opened.

Hope walked away from her. "I wish you wouldn't call me that."

"What? You wish I wouldn't tell you that you look like shit?"

"You know what I mean."

"When are you coming back to the house?" Janelle asked, following her into the house without waiting for a formal invitation.

"I don't know."

"We need you. That house is falling apart without you and Mr. Sam."

Hope laughed; not in a joyful way, but in a mean, spiteful manner. "Well, Mr. Sam is otherwise occupied."

Janelle wasn't going to let her get away with being flippant and evasive. "You need to get it together. We are all sad about Mr. Sam, but he would want you to carry on the Hope House."

"I'm not ready."

"Well, that's not good enough." Janelle put her hand on Hope's shoulder, which was bony and meatless. Grief wasn't a hungry beast. "You come back and let the work heal you. That's the only way to survive."

As much as Hope had wanted to argue and ignore Janelle's point, it was pointless because she knew that returning to the Hope House was the answer. Staying in her home was a no longer an option. Although the shelter was a part of her and Sam's life together it didn't hold quite the same memories or connections that the rooms in their three-bedroom bungalow held. If Hope had any chance of floating along in life, she had to pull up the anchor. Three days after Janelle begged her to let the Hope House resuscitate her, a "for sale" sign went up in the front yard and Hope moved into the shelter.

She allowed the shelter and the kids to slowly reintroduce her to the land of the living, while she worked tirelessly building living quarters for herself so she could have some privacy. She and Sam had never been able to have children, although they had both wanted them. Sam had suggested adoption, but Hope balked at the idea. She wasn't sure she was capable of raising someone else's child. Her mother may have made it seem easy, but there were still those moments of awareness and clarity that made it quite obvious that a biological schism existed. Sam had accepted her reasoning without argument and never pressed her on the issue. Instead, they took pride in offering a temporary home to as many young adults that needed it and built their own distinctive family. How could she have known that by coming back to the shelter instead of abandoning it in her grief that her life would be colored a different shade once again?

\*\*\*

Fate has a way of barging into one's life, intervening in the oddest and most uncomfortable ways imaginable. It can actually be quite rude; not waiting its turn, but instead insisting on being given consideration and ample time to present its case. Hope had never quite believed in fate. On the scale of being an overrated notion, it ranked near the top next to Santa and God. It wasn't that Hope hadn't been witness to miracles and plot teasers in her life that one could comfortably attribute to destiny; she just never wanted to be at its mercy or in its debt. She didn't want to owe her good fortune to anyone but herself. On the flipside, she didn't want to fall into that trap of blaming all her bad luck on some entity or notion, refusing to take responsibility for bad choices and missed opportunities.

Regardless of what Hope believed or didn't believe about fate, she couldn't deny that every decision of her life had led her to this one moment when the doorbell at Hope House rang on a Sunday morning in mid-January of 2010. On the front step stood a woman she would have known in an instant. Words didn't have to be spoken. Proof didn't have to be presented. The proof, the evidence, the truth, lingered in the air connecting the two women by an invisible string that no sharp object could have ever severed.

## Chapter 25 – Charlotte
*Present Day*

"She visited you?" I asked, completely stunned that my mother had traveled all the way from Marion to visit this stranger. Of course, she wasn't really a stranger was she? She had inhabited my mother's womb for nine months. You don't get more familiar than that.

"Yes, about seven months ago." Hope answered.

"Did she tell you she was dying?" Again Hope answered affirmatively. Jealousy and anger turned my body cold. How was this possible? How was it at all conceivable that my mother could have given this woman time to come to terms with her death, but ignored me and pushed me aside? As if reading my thoughts, Hope tried to offer an explanation.

"She just wanted to see me. That was all. She didn't want anything. She wasn't here to replace you, Charlotte."

Hearing my name roll of her tone in such a casual way fueled the anger and jealousy. I hadn't even told her my name. "She told you my name."

Hope smiled. "Of course, she told me all about you. She was very proud of you. She said you were a big-shot marketing guru up in the big city. Chicago, right?"

I didn't know what to say. I thought that by coming here I had it all figured out. I would gently break the news to this woman that I was her half-sibling and provide her with comfort, telling her that our mother had passed. Instead it was the opposite. Again, I was the last one to know. While I sat in a winged back chair, listening to the sounds of Spongebob Square Pants echoing through the vents, Harold spoke.

"Did she talk about me?" he asked. "Did she tell you about your father?"

Hope drew her breath in, taking a moment before she answered. "We spoke more about her and her life."

"So she said nothing about me?"

"I knew your name. I asked her for your name, but that was all she provided. I'm sorry. Truly, I am sorry. You seem like a good man."

"A good man wouldn't have existed on this planet for as long as I have not knowing he had a daughter," Harold mumbled.

"It happens," Hope responded in a matter of fact kind of way. "At least you didn't know. There are kids that walk through this door all the time that are purposely abandoned by their parents. It's not the same as not knowing and it doesn't make you a bad man."

Harold looked down at his shoes, accepting and rejecting her answer at the same time. She then addressed me. "What do you want to know, Charlotte? I'm sorry that I tried to turn you away. I saw your car pull up," she indicated the window behind me that looked down over the street. "When you got out I recognized you immediately." She reached into her desk drawer and pulled out a picture from mine and Nick's wedding. "Your mother gave this to me. Such a beautiful bride and the groom isn't too bad either." She hesitated then continued, "I just didn't know what I was supposed to say or do. That's why I asked Janelle to send you away."

"Everything," I said. "I want to know everything. I came here for answers, but now I have more questions. What did my mother say to you? Did she explain herself?" The words were falling fast from my lips.

"To a point," Hope said. "It was hard for her; hard for me. Just like it is hard for both of you right now."

"Tell me," I demanded. "Tell me everything."

## Chapter 26 – Francis "Hope" McCabe
*Seven Months Earlier*

Hope offered her tea, coffee, water, whatever she had, but the woman shook her head. They both stood in the kitchen of the shelter studying each other from opposite sides of the ginormous prepping island. The woman, she said her name was Sylvie, was about five inches shorter than she was. It made Hope feel like a giant. She assumed she'd gotten her height from her father.

"I apologize for surprising you," Sylvie had said. "I should have called."

Hope didn't agree or disagree. Would it have been better to have been warned? Probably not, she decided. Instead, she asked, "Why are you here?"

Sylvie motioned towards the kitchen table. "May I sit? It was a long plane ride and the cab driver was a horrible motorist. I am exhausted."

Hope pulled out a chair for the woman, for her mother. Should she even say that word? Wasn't that betraying her parents even if they had both been dead and buried for so many years?

Sylvie sat and continued, not mincing any words. "I'm dying. I needed to see you."

"It's that simple?" Hope asked.

Sylvie chuckled, uncomfortably. "Yes. It's that simple. Or,

extremely complicated. Whichever way you look at it doesn't change the situation, I suppose."

"Dying from what?"

"Glioblastoma, it's a brain cancer."

Hope's heart had quickened. "Is it hereditary?"

"Thankfully, no. There doesn't seem to be any sort of genetic disposition."

"How long?"

"Doctors say about three months, but I have some good doctors and some treatment options. I think I can squeeze a few more months out of that prognosis."

Hope didn't know what to say. It seemed cruel that after 57 years she would finally get to meet the woman whose genes she shared, who birthed her, to arrive carrying a death announcement. Sam would have said it was ironic, but Hope didn't quite know what to call it. They both sat at the table silent, the tick-tock, tick-tock rhythm of the clock keeping the beat of the silence.

"I came to see you once," Sylvie confessed. "So many years ago that sometimes it seems more like a dream than something that actually happened. You were five. I had just finished my undergraduate degree and I was trying to decide between finding you or continuing with my education. I boarded a bus and headed this way, hoping the long ride would clear my head and give me direction."

"How did you know where to find me?"

Sylvie pursed her lips and looked away as if she were ashamed of what she was about to admit. "It was an open adoption. The nuns at the orphanage told me that if I ever wanted to know where you were they would provide me with the information."

"I see."

"Your – " she paused then continued. "Your mother found me watching you in the schoolyard. She had just walked you to school and was leaving. She asked me to walk away. To make peace with my decision and to leave you be. She told me she was giving you love, that you didn't want for anything, and that she was your mother. How could I argue with that?"

"My mother never told me I was adopted."

"You didn't act surprised when you opened the door."

"Just because she never verbalized that I wasn't her biological child doesn't mean that I didn't sense it."

Sylvie nodded. She reached into her purse and pulled out a picture of a much younger woman. "This is your sister."

Hope studied the photograph. It was surreal to finally see a family photograph where she could discern a genetic presence. In a way this young woman looked a lot like Hope had at that age, with a few exceptions, because she was quite certain they didn't share the same father. "She's pretty. What's her name?"

"Charlotte."

"Her father?" Hope asked just to be sure.

Sylvie shook her head. "Not the same. Her father, my husband, he died when she was just two."

Hope handed her the picture back, but Sylvie shook her head. "Please keep it."

"My husband passed away two years ago." Hope didn't know quite why she said this. Maybe it was out of a need to share something that went beyond blood type and hair color.

"Did you two have children?"

Hope shook her head and saw the woman's face fall a bit. "No. We were never able to."

"Charlotte has struggled with having children, too. There has been much sadness in that part of her life for her and Nick. That's her husband's name."

"Does she know about me?" Hope asked.

Sylvie shook her head. "No one does."

"What about my father?"

"I never told him."

"You should," Hope said. "He probably has a right to know."

"Maybe," Sylvie said. "Maybe not. I never loved him."

"There are many children born that aren't conceived out of love." Hope nodded in the direction of the living room. "I see it every day. What's his name?"

"Harold Klein. I never listed him on the birth certificate, but you're right. You have a right to know. So does he."

"You should tell her, too." Hope insisted.

"Charlotte? She's fragile. She's had a lot happen to her. She's gotten stronger over the years, but something like this might undo everything she has worked so hard for."

"How is she coping with your diagnosis?" Sylvie hugged her purse tighter to her body, not answering her directly, but letting her muteness provide the response.

"Sometimes people are stronger than they know. You should probably give her more credit," Hope said gently.

"I've run away from a lot in my life. I'm sorry for that. But I'm not sure I can run to my daughter and tell her about my lies, my death. It's better to let things be, don't you think?"

"Are you asking me not to say anything?" Hope asked.

"I guess once the earth is dug and my body is lowered into the trenches that decision is out of my hands. But, yes, I suppose that is what I am asking you."

After that there was nothing left to say. The women sat at the table each contemplating their circumstances, until after a few moments of silence Sylvie pushed her chair back and moved to leave. Her voice cracked as she delivered her farewell. "So much I have done wrong. So many mistakes. But you and Charlotte have been my greatest accomplishments. I am glad I got to lay eyes on you. I'm glad I got to meet you."

## Chapter 27 – Charlotte
*Present Day*

The only one in the room not crying was Harold, which I suspected was only because of his pride. Pride may make one turn to stone on the outside, but it doesn't stop the weeping of the heart.

"Thank you," I said because I didn't know what else to say.

"When did she pass away?" Hope asked.

"Last Sunday."

"I don't know what to say to you, Charlotte. Or even you, Harold. There is probably so much to say, which is why this seems rather difficult."

"Family is complicated," I offered.

Hope smiled. "You aren't lying about that. You know I always wanted a sister."

I grinned, feeling a little lighter. "Me, too."

"My brothers were – are – great, but it's just not the same. Plus, they always smelled like dirty socks and armpit stain."

Harold cleared his throat and reached into his back pocket, his hands shaking from what I suspected was a combination of age and fear. From the innards of the billfold he produced a few wallet-sized photos. He handed them to Hope.

"These here are your grandparents. Been deceased for many years, but I think if you look closely you'll see a resemblance between you and my mother. And," he leaned forward pointing to another person, "that's my twin sister, Mabel. Thankfully, you look nothing like her." Father and daughter laughed together. "You can keep those."

"What about you, Harold?" Hope asked. "Did you have any children?"

"My Isabel and I weren't lucky in that department. Sounds like it runs in the family, " he said. "Well, you know what I mean."

I touched Harold's knee and winked at him, explaining to Hope. "He's kind of an insensitive jerk, but once you get to know him he's not that bad."

Hope laughed again. "That runs in the family, too."

When the laughter died out the conversation stalled. I didn't know what was left to say. It may have been better if I had come with a plan, but instead I came on a whim. I just needed to see this other person. I hadn't intended to like her or want to form a relationship with her, but I knew as soon as I had locked eyes with her that I wouldn't be able to let her go. If anything, she was an extension of my mother, but she was also a part of me. She was someone I wanted this child I was carrying to know.

Again, as if reading my mind, Hope spoke. "I don't have much to offer. What you see is what you get. My life's here and I'm not going to leave it. But I would very much like to stay in contact with you."

"I would like that very much," I said.

Hope turned to Harold. "I never came looking for you or Sylvie because I felt like it would be disloyal to my mother and father. But that doesn't mean that I don't welcome you into my life, too. I regret that I didn't ask Sylvie to stay. It pains me more than I can express that I let her walk out of my life a second time, but it doesn't have to be that way with us. Nobody is too old to have a father."

Those words were the chisel that broke the stone that encased Harold's body. For the second time in as many days, Harold sobbed. Tears fell from my eyes, too, as I watched Hope and Harold embrace. For a split second jealousy churned in my stomach, but it dissipated just as quickly because this is what Mom had wanted.

She may have not been able to make things right with Harold. She may have never been able to forgive herself for walking away from her child. Sylvie Day may have lived every day with the remorse and shame for the choices she made that shaped so many lives, but none of that mattered now. In the end, she brought together a family because that is who my mother was. My mom had spent her entire existence in the waiting room, not sure if the news would be good or bad. Not sure if introducing her child to her family would be welcome news or contribute to the loss of her family's trust. In the end, she needn't have worried. Bringing us together meant new life was breathed into the broken and pieced back together lives of me, Harold, and even Hope. In this way her presence remained with us and a part of our lives.

## Epilogue

### *Charlotte - October 2012*

The sun was setting earlier and earlier every day. The long shadows that fell across the fields of green and brown were noticeable around five o'clock now. These were the days that I loved most. The air was chilly in the evening, but still warm during the day. It made it difficult to figure out how to dress Sophie. She didn't like clothes that much as it was, so getting her dressed to begin with was a challenge, but we managed.

It was hard to believe that she turned two back in March. During my pregnancy I had dismissed the more experienced parents I ran into during childbirth classes and other pre-natal events who had insisted that time sped up once the pain of labor went away. They warned me not to blink because before I knew it she would be crawling, then walking, then getting married. Yes, it really does happen that fast, they swore. I humored these strange creatures – parents – swearing to Nick that they were melodramatic and down-right wrong. Time was not something that could be sped up or slowed down; being a parent didn't change that. Turns out I was the foolish one for believing in something as fickle as time.

The past two years had flown by. Sophie ran me ragged all day long. I couldn't believe that one little girl could have so much energy.

Nick had suggested we get a dog. "To keep her company and take her for runs."

"Runs? Isn't she supposed to take the dog for walks?" I asked one evening when we were sitting on the porch of the farmhouse watching Sophie chase her shadow.

"Have you met our child? She's kind of an animal herself."

I rested my head on Nick's shoulder and counted my blessings. It had been a little more than two years since Mom died. Every day I missed her and the pain never really did go away. It wasn't as glaring and some days it took until I had my first cup of coffee in the morning for me to remember that she wasn't in the living room reading from her books or journals. Those God-awful boring medical journals were still lying on top of the bookshelves, but I couldn't get rid of them.

When Mom died and I was left motherless and pregnant, I felt so alone. But the moment that Nick and I brought Sophie into the world at 3:21 am on March 1, 2011, in the middle of a not-so-rare late winter snowstorm, I knew that I would never be lonely again. Sophie completed me and brought me closer to my mom than I had ever thought was possible.

The three of us had spent the first three months of Sophie's life in our city home, but it became quite obvious to me that it was time to make a change. The farmhouse had been sitting vacant, gathering dust while I decided what to do with the property. Selling it would have netted us a nice bundle for Sophie's college or our retirement, but the idea of selling that property was unbearable. Then one evening after Sophie had taken her bath and the three of us were nestled on the sofa trying to block out the city noise, Nick made a bold suggestion.

"Let's move."

"Move where?"

"To the farmhouse."

"That's not a move across town or to the suburbs. That's a move – move. We'd be leaving everything behind. What about your job?"

Nick stroked Sophie's nose as he explained. "With the

farmhouse paid for we only have to worry about taxes. We won't have a house payment and the cost of living is so much cheaper in Marion. And with Harold gone, he said I could use the office space for my own practice."

I regarded him closely. "Harold? When did you speak with him?"

"Last week. Come on, Charlie. You know I don't make wild and crazy suggestions without researching every angle first. I *am* a lawyer."

***

After our initial meeting with Hope, as we were walking back to the car, Harold had told me his plans. "I'm staying," he had said.

"Here?"

He nodded. "There's nothing back home that I can't find here. They have stores, food, water, shelter. I think I'd like to stay here."

"What about your family?" I had asked.

"Mabel? That woman can take care of herself. And if not, she has a whole brood of children and grandchildren to help her. I want to stay here and get to know my daughter. Who knows how much time I have left?"

"I think that's a wonderful idea, but are you sure you can get used to the clothing choices down here? I thought Florida was for pansies?"

Harold smiled. "What do I know? Maybe you can teach an old dog new tricks. Perhaps I'll look good in a flowery shirt. I might even wear shorts."

Harold had done well in Florida. Living in a warmer climate that didn't constantly remind him of his failures and lost opportunities back home had lifted his spirits. The last time I talked to him he had even gotten a part-time job at the local Wal-Mart as a greeter, which was surprising on a number of levels.

***

Once Nick explained the logic behind his suggestion to move back to Marion, I couldn't argue. It made perfect sense and I have never regretted the move. While small town life may not have agreed with me as a teenager, it soothed me now.

Since meeting Hope we have stayed in touch, mostly via technology: the phone, texts, social media, and the occasional Skype session. She hasn't visited yet and I'm not sure that she ever will. I try not to let this bother me because I can't imagine being in her place and juggling the feelings that go with knowing she is the product of two families; one created from blood, the other created from yearning. She seems happy where she is and I think that is enough.

If there is anything I have learned since losing my mother, it is that we all carry pain, burden, and shame. Some carry more than others and have more to lose, but it doesn't really matter because shame is shame. However, when you let those feelings of remorse and unworthiness go, the world actually welcomes you with open arms. It doesn't continue to scold you. It doesn't continue to remind you of who you once were. Instead, it wraps itself around you like a warm blanket, making it possible for you to believe in yourself again.

I hope my mom is in a warm, safe place. I hope that she is watching over me, Nick, and her granddaughter; proud of the little family we have made. I couldn't have ever asked for a better life than the one I had with my mom in this little farmhouse. I can only hope that I am able to give that same life to my daughter and be half the woman that she was.

# ACKNOWLEDGEMENTS

This is the part of the book where I get to say thank you and bestow praise and gratitude to everyone who has helped along this amazing journey that has had too many potholes to count. It is the Oscar speech for the novelist.

So, let me get started by thanking my family, especially my mother and father who were the early champions of my career when I had purchased a $90 Smith Corona typewriter and spent too many hours in locked away from the world writing about worlds I had no idea about.

To my husband who has continuously nudged and pushed me in the direction of fulfilling the dream to become a published writer with a book that can be displayed on our bookshelves along with fabulous writers like Stephen King, Amy Tan, Barbara Kingsolver, and so many more I couldn't begin to name. Also, thank you to my daughters who inspire me to keep reaching new heights and taking chances.

Of course, I can't forget to thank my editor, Kristina, who helped me create a story I can be proud of. A huge thank you to my last-minute savior, Marty, for creating the cover layout and putting his creative skills to work at a moment's notice to get me out of a bind and to Raq A

Bye Photography for sharing her sweet, baby photos with me.

Lastly, but certainly not least in any way, thank you to all my current and future readers. The written word means so much to me and to not be able to share my stories with you would be a tragedy.

## ABOUT PIPER PUNCHES

Piper Punches lives in the far west suburbs of St. Louis with her husband and two daughters. *The Waiting Room* is her debut novel. Piper is excited to connect with her readers and encourages everyone to stop by her website and say hello. In the meantime, she is currently working a short novella, *Missing Girl*, available January 2014.

## CONNECT WITH PIPER PUNCHES
www.piperpunches.com
www.facebook.com/piperpunches
www.twitter.com/piperpunches
www.goodreads.com/piperpunches

# MISSING GIRL

In life my name was Sophia Lucia Cruz. In death it is simply *missing girls*. Not even singular, but plural, as if there was never one single part of me that was unique or separate from all the other girls that were buried in that harsh Mexican dirt; victims of circumstance, irrevocable choices, and just plain bad luck. If I still had the capacity to cry, I would, because it is that sad and tragic. But when the knife slid deep into my belly and the blood gurgled at the base of my throat I knew that tears wouldn't save me and they won't change my story now.

Why am I here? You don't believe in ghosts, do you? That's okay. I didn't either before I became one. Even when I was a little girl and I insisted I saw my *abuela's* ghost at the foot of my bed, knitting me a blanket that had all the colors of the rainbow, I let myself be persuaded that ghosts were a figment of my imagination.

"Sophia," my mama said as she smoothed my hair and planted her lips on my head. "My sweet Sophia, close your eyes. Whatever you think you saw was a shadow. Just a trick of the moon." She would then sing me a song and rock me back to sleep.

I wish I could visit mama at the foot of her bed tonight. I wish I could tell her this isn't her fault. She did the best she could. She should forgive herself. But I can't. Instead I am stuck here; wherever here is. It's somewhere between the dark black Mexican night and its brilliant sunny days. I am simply hovering above what remains of my body. People, family members, loved ones, sometimes the police, make their way to these dusty fields with picks, sticks, and shovels, hopping to discover the remains of their missing girl, but most of them find nothing and end up leaving the fields more distraught than when they arrived. Isn't it twisted the way that families are forced to come to these fields of death with hope and expectations of finding their loved ones? I am not judging and I certainly don't blame them. But when they leave they leave hopeless because they know that they will continue to be left without answers - without a body to properly bury. Because let's face it: when the missing leave they never return.

I'm there. I can see me - or at least what is left of me. Some of the girls – and men, too – that are buried (can you even call it that?) here were merely stabbed, shot, choked, or suffocated and then haphazardly tossed like garbage into this death dump. Not me. Although no one would come looking for me and I wasn't anyone important, my kidnappers had left their marks branded on my skin and this made me identifiable and a risk even in death. Unlike some of the other bodies buried around me, I was dug a deep enough grave that I wouldn't be noticed right away. This would give the lime that had been sprinkled over my body time to work its decomposing magic.

How can I talk about my demise so casually? I don't know. Perhaps that is the beauty of death. I am removed not only from my physical body, but my emotions are flat-lined as well. However, I still feel compelled to tell my story, so there must be some emotion that lingers, even though my soul has released its grip on my human form.

Why am I compelled to tell this story? I guess because no one else will. Most people don't want to tell stories with tragic endings, but they need to be told, otherwise they are forgotten. I want you to know who I am. I want you to know I am so much more than a poster that has been damaged by wind, rain, and time. I don't want to be so easily dismissed. I want you to know that I was so much more than a missing girl.

## READ MORE

## Want to Read Missing Girl for Free?

## SIGN UP HERE

http://eepurl.com/baITVz

Titles by Piper Punches

The Waiting Room
Missing Girl
Legacy, An Anthology

And, coming soon. . .

Girls go missing every day and disappear never to be heard from again. Some are missed. Most are forgotten. Another missing girl is what authorities told her Emily when her twin sister, Lizzie, disappears while chasing a past that threatens to destroy them forever. Emily won't accept this. Letting go of her sister is not an option, but time is running out and Emily has a secret of her own.

*60 Days* takes the reader into the depths of darkness where women are treated as commodities to be used over and over again. This boldly written, psychological thriller will leave you wondering, *How far would you go to rescue someone you love from the depths of hell?*

## 60 DAYS
**Coming Soon**

Piper Punches

Made in the USA
Charleston, SC
08 November 2015